THE

FAIRKIND

A novel by
Randolph Kuczer

Published by Skipper House LLC, Panama City Beach, FL
First edition. April 2025

Scripture quotations taken from The Holy Bible,
New International Version® NIV®
Copyright © 1973, 1978, 1984, 2011 by Biblica, Inc.
Used with permission. All rights reserved worldwide.

Publisher's Cataloging-in-Publication Data
Names: Kuczer, Randolph, author.
Title: The Fairkind / Randolph Kuczer.
Series: The Fairkind
Description: Panama City Beach, FL: Skipper House, LLC, 2025.
Identifiers: LCCN: 2025902084 | ISBN: 979-8-9925546-0-1 (print) | 979-8-9925546-1-8 (ebook)
Subjects: LCSH Fairies--Fiction. | Magic--Fiction. | Oregon--Fiction. | Coming of age--Fiction. | Romance fiction. | Fantasy fiction. | BISAC YOUNG ADULT FICTION / Fantasy / Contemporary | YOUNG ADULT FICTION / Fantasy / Romance
Classification: LCC PS3611 .U35 Fa 2025 | DDC 813.6--dc23

ISBN: 979-8-9925546-0-1
eBook ISBN: 979-8-9925546-1-8

Printed in the United States of America

Cover art by VannGo Designs

For inquiries, contact the author at: kuczer.randolph@gmail.com

"As iron sharpens iron, so one person sharpens another."

PROVERBS 27:17 - NIV

ONE

HER VOICE SCRAPES MY EARS like there's a sandstorm in her windpipe. "He'll be here any minute. The others, too."

"Yes, Mother. I won't let them in," I say, trying to convince myself I'm not afraid of them. I spread an extra quilt over her covers and tuck her in tightly, hoping it's enough to keep her warm. The temperature has already dropped considerably.

Even a forewarning doesn't stop me from being startled as three bangs strike the front door. The whole house shakes. And I can't tell if it's from the storm or the pounding fist against the wood. I'm used to it, though. Our house is built into the sturdy branches of an old oak. It's usually comforting to sway with the movement of the tree, but not tonight.

"Jane," a muffled, gruff voice sounds from outside. The squall hasn't deterred *him* and his heavy fist. Fear prickles through me as I slink closer and crack the door ajar.

Artifice, the Elder of tempting—my least favorite of the five Offerings granted to our kind—has dropped by unannounced many times over the past few months. He always insists on seeing

Mother, but she refuses. Now all five Elders stand before me, torches in hand. Their faces as stiff as their cloaks. *Here we go again.*

Artifice is the tallest, standing head and shoulders above the rest. The torchlight illuminates his sunken eyes and hollowed cheeks, bringing some much-needed color to his face. He is over one hundred and fifty years old and even yearly healings can't help it from showing. His thick, white hair is slicked back, and a red cloak falls crisply over his thin frame.

Herald stands fittingly abreast with Artifice's right side. Everything about him is impish. He always looks particularly uncomfortable in his stocky frame. And this time is no exception, as he cranes what little neck he has toward the crack in the door.

The other Elders, Curative, Ginger, and Gust stand further back near the porch railing, surely having been dragged along to make it seem more official. Gust's large palms point outward from his waist, using his Offering to shield us from the downpour. He's big and muscular, but his kind eyes make him less fearsome than Artifice and Herald. "Why don't you send the storm off altogether?" I ask him.

"We don't like to meddle with nature unless we must. But how about a compromise?" Even elevated, his voice is calm and controlled. He waves his hands purposefully and drops them back to his sides. The dark clouds above jolt outward, halting the rain, but only around our oak.

Mother used to be one of them, and the Elders know just how powerful she is. Foreseers can typically see impending events with clarity or distant, obscure things. But none see the depths of the future as clearly as she does. Elders are forbidden to have distractions from their duties—such as children or a spouse. So, when she got pregnant with me, she resigned from her Eldership and never looked back. This worked out well for her successor, Herald. The putz would have never been a contender otherwise.

2

Mother says she doesn't regret it. That it was all part of the plan. But our kind doesn't have illegitimate children. It is unheard of. And sadly, all family ties were severed as a result. As for my father, I know nothing of him. I suspect I never will.

The Elders are silent as they peer past my slight frame, scanning the dim family room behind me. I stare at Artifice with anxious eyes, cocking my head until his gaze finally shifts to meet mine. "To what do I owe the pleasure of such esteemed guests on this dreadful night?" I ask, trying to keep my voice from shaking.

Nervous beads of sweat form along Herald's receding hairline. "Don't act surprised to see us," he snaps. An unfortunate tuft of hair stands at attention while the rest of his black hair cowers near his scalp. That tuft might lie flat if he grew his hair out a bit more, but I'd never suggest it to him.

Artifice places a firm hand on Herald's shoulder, quieting him, and leans in closer to me. "Dreadful indeed. How is Sibyl faring?" The sharp scent of mint rolls off his breath, stinging my nostrils. *Ew. That's not doing much for the lingering odor from your last meal.*

"Still unwell. But I suspect you already know that," I say, eyeing Herald carefully.

Mother always says, "Herald can't see his own two feet, let alone the future!" Even so, I'm sure he has the foresight to know she's nearing the end. Even I know that, and I don't have an Offering yet.

"Curative needs to heal her before it is too late," Artifice says, budging the door open wider with his bony elbow. His eyes dart around me, presumably searching for any sign of her. Curative's thin lips curl into a sincere half-smile.

"Go away!" Mother booms from her bedroom.

I wince at her sharp tone. "I'm sorry. She doesn't want your help." I battle Artifice to shut the door.

Herald holds out his stumpy hand to keep the door from closing. "Wait–Jane, please. I know Sibyl is stubborn, but you can save her. What will you do if something happens to her? You would be all alone."

This is an obvious attempt to exploit my emotions. I hate to admit that it's almost working. "Don't pretend you've come out of concern for me," I say, doubling down against the door.

Artifice leans into Herald. "You're certain it will happen tonight?" he says just above a whisper.

"Yes, I saw it," Herald says.

"You've been wrong before," Artifice mumbles under his breath, still wrestling with the door.

Herald raises his voice, "I said I'm certain!"

Artifice clicks his tongue. His long, narrow nose points at me. "*Are you sure you won't let us in, then?*" he asks, eyes locked on me. I feel woozy the instant the words leave his lips. His voice echoes persuasively in my head. My pulse quickens as my legs unwillingly shuffle backward. My knuckles turn white, clenching tightly around the doorknob and I yank it open wide.

Ginger stomps her foot. "That's enough, Artifice! She's just a girl." Her orange bob of hair shakes. Artifice snaps his head to glower at Ginger, and suddenly I'm released from his influence.

I feel humiliated. Violated. He has no right to enter my mind. To probe my thoughts. To will me into submission. I quickly close the door back to a crack. "Stay out of my head, Artifice! Just leave us alone!" I shriek at him.

"My apologies for the intrusion," he grumbles, narrowing his eyes.

"If they want our help, they know where to find us," Ginger snaps. Her voice is firm. She turns to face me. "If you or your mother need anything, please don't hesitate to ask. We are always here." I force a smile and nod. If it were up to me, I'd honestly let them in. But Mother has made it very clear that she does not wish to be healed. And she knows so much more than I do. More than any of them, too.

"Thank you for checking on us...*again*," I say.

The Elders go down the narrow stairway toward the ground, but Artifice hangs back a moment longer. His face twists into a scowl. "What a waste," he says.

I clench a fist at my side, slam the door shut, and march into Mother's room just as the rain hammers back down. "They just want to help you. Why won't you let them?" I blubber in confusion.

"Don't be foolish, Jane," she says with a cough, struggling to sit up in her bed.

"You never tell me anything! I'm not a child anymore!"

Her forehead wrinkles. "Come here," she says, holding out her feeble hand. I edge closer and lock hands with her. "Great danger comes from knowing tomorrow."

"What kind of danger? I don't understand."

"I don't expect you to understand. I expect you to trust me." A mist slides over the blue of her eyes, and she smiles.

"What do you see now?" I ask, more irritably than I should have.

"Kismet," she says wistfully.

"Like fate?"

"Yes. Very much so." She yawns and sinks back under the covers. She's ambiguous in her choice of words, and frequently so. One of the problems with having the ability to see the future is the risk of altering it. Even a simple slip of the tongue, negligible to say the least, can change the succeeding course of events. That's what she tells me anyway.

"I'd love to daydream with you, but someone's got to start on dinner. Do you need anything else before I go?"

"No, dear. Thank you."

I prepare some oatmeal with cinnamon, just the way Mother prefers it. It's still quite hot when I teeter back into her room with the bowl. I blow the steam across the surface and hear her strain a snore. I set the bowl down and lean over to examine her breathing. Shallow, but steady.

The candles have fizzled out in pools of wax, but the zaps of lightning are frequent enough to see. I stare down at the rough texture her skin now carries which is rare for our kind. Rumors swirl of the humans being prone to the same affliction as they age, but I have never seen one to know if that's true. The silence is broken by the coarse, wet crackles she coughs from deep in her lungs. I reach for her hands. "Mother?"

"Yes, dear," she says between labored gasps.

"Curative might still be outside. I'll go try to find her."

She grabs me by the hand. "No…" Her wrinkles deepen as a smile tugs at her lips. "Do you have any idea how important you are?"

I plant a soft kiss on her cheek, grazing my nose against her skin. "I love you," I breathe between soft sobs.

"And I…you." Her grip slowly weakens until it goes limp. A blinding flash of light bursts through the room and it's as if shadows have never been attached to any of the objects therein.

"NO! DON'T TAKE HER!" I cry as I squeeze tighter around her cold fingers, trying to keep her there. But the light ignores my cries and surges from her, spreading through her body like wildfire. I jerk my hand back to shield my eyes, despite how compelled I am to gaze at its splendor. Behind the veil of my fingertips, I watch her frail frame slowly lift and condense into a bright orb. Then she's gone, and the empty room fills with darkness once again.

TWO

A S THE WORST SUMMER OF my life comes to an end, I am somewhat hopeful for what comes next for me—my Offering. I wake up early to bathe in the small brook near the house and race to school, determined to not be late for my first day.

The ground crunches under my boots until I stop in my tracks, staring up at the height of a gargantuan redwood tree. A staircase spirals around the large trunk, high into the treetops. I exhale a shaky breath and start the climb. Each step up seems to be followed by a hundred more as I scale the never-ending stairs to the main deck, perched midway up the tree.

The deck stands central to five other redwoods that each house a classroom. They are some of the oldest and largest redwoods in the forest. Each tree has a rickety bridge that converges at the central landing. The Redwoods are considerably taller than the cluster of low-lying trees of primary school at the Oaks, my only school until now. I have never been this high before, still, the sweat from my palms and my reluctance to look down surprises me.

I zigzag through the buzzing crowd over to the railing to admire the lush, panoramic view. The forest is just starting to come alive for a new day. "Ahem!" a melodious voice rings out from behind me. I avert my gaze from the wilderness. Fairmaster Lily stands before the crowd, waiting patiently for everyone's attention. Plenty of gossip from the Redwoods trickles down to the Oaks but only nice things are said about her. She's that one Fairmaster everyone wishes they could have. Sadly, I'm not a grower, so I already know that she won't be mine.

Fairmaster Lily is tall and slender, her pale skin looking fresh against her dress of cotton. A pair of brilliant blue eyes twinkle above her pink cheeks, and a band of white and purple flowers adorns her head. I can't help but envy her golden waves as she nervously runs her fingers through them. *What I wouldn't give to be a blond. But no, had to be the color of bear scat. As if my life isn't rough enough.*

Her eyes dart around the noisy horde a few more moments before she bellows out, "Welcome, students, to your first day at the Redwoods! I trust you had a pleasant summer. Now that you are all seventeen, the time has come for you to learn how to wield your Offerings, as you will soon enter adulthood. The training you receive here will prepare you to carry out the Trials successfully. This will secure your position among the Fairkind. Afterward, you will be appointed to your new work post." Fairmaster Lily breaks off as the students start to whisper, then clears her throat again and continues:

"Each of you has a destiny set before you, a destiny that was predicted when you were infants, and it is here you will develop the Offering you were born with." Her smooth voice echoes as she gestures to each of the five massive trees surrounding the landing. "Each school day, you are to report to the class of your Offering–tempting, conditioning, growing, foreseeing, and healing. Your assigned Fairmaster will instruct you for the duration of your training. I am pleased to be returning this year for my forty-third term as your Grower Fairmaster!"

Cheers erupt from a small section of students, who I can only assume are growers. "Let's get started. Growers! Follow me. Everyone else, head to your class. Have a wonderful first day!" she says. We all hurry toward the hanging bridges that lead into the five classrooms. Framing the bridges are large pillars on either side, each supporting a hefty, raw gemstone. I pay close attention to the stones, making sure not to enter the wrong class.

A lump forms in my throat as I pass the bridge of diamonds. That would have been Mother's class many years ago—the foreseers. I wonder what might have been running through her mind on her first day at the Redwoods. Probably nothing like the grief I'm feeling. *So, don't think about it.*

I slow to a stop and stand before the bridge of rubies. This is it. I inhale deeply and follow behind the other students when they move. My hands grip tightly around the support ropes as the bridge sways under us. It's a long fall to the ground below.

A cheesy banner that reads, "Tempting is Terrifyingly Terrific!" is stuck to the front door of the classroom, and there are plenty of equally trite posters on the walls inside. The student desks are arranged in tight rows, but the Fairmaster's desk is strewn with messy stacks of parchment held down by chunks of rubies for parchmentweights. You would think the school year was near completion by the chaos, instead of just beginning.

A petite woman stands centered at the front of the room. She waits for everyone to quiet and lowers the hood of the black robe tied firmly around her waist. Her sleek, black hair falls just below her shoulders with swooping bangs. Short in stature as she stands, her dark eyes bore into you, making you feel even smaller than she is.

I've been around tempters before, sure, but never too close. The thought of someone being able to control my mind has always been unsettling. I tell myself I'm not scared of them, but it's stupid. I am. Artifice's stunt over the summer was just a minor example from a lengthy list of their distasteful exploits. So, I have always kept my distance, even though I am destined to join them.

The class creates a half-circle around the Fairmaster, not leaving much wiggle room for me to sink to the back. "How was your summer, *Plain Jane*?" A shrill voice startles me from behind. *"Plain Jane with the strangest name."* The cruel chant from my childhood still rings in my ears.

I turn, knowing full well who said it. *Wow.* Duplicity is barely recognizable from the lanky girl with freckles she had been last year. Summer was good to her. She now stands stunning, completely filled out with gleaming green eyes and voluminous red hair.

Duplicity is a bully in every sense of the word. And apparently, she isn't going to cut me any slack, even if Mother did just pass away. Perhaps she doesn't know. But I wouldn't put it past her to torment me if she did. It's not surprising for a tempter to have a wicked streak, but she takes it to extremes.

I shrug her off with a small smirk and turn back to face the front. I want to pay attention, anything to distract me from the gaping hole in my heart. But the more I focus on the Fairmaster, the more I notice how peculiar her eyes are. Their depths are infinite. They suck me in, like a pool of quicksand.

My eyes remain trained on the Fairmaster as Duplicity lunges past me for a spot closer to the front but, with a sudden jerk, I thrust my foot into her path. She stumbles over my outstretched boot and falls to her knees with a loud smack. My eyes widen in horror, as the fog of magic disperses from my mind. I quickly bend down to help her up, but she swats my hand away, her cheeks now matching her red hair.

The entire room falls silent. Duplicity is the last person anyone wants to cross. This is understood. My peers exchange fearful glances, then look at me for an explanation, to which I have none. *Umm. What just happened?*

The Fairmaster sneers, "At least put up a fight next time I try that, Jane. You let me right in." I haven't met this woman before, but one uninvited gaze into my mind tells her everything she could ever hope to know about me. "And this, class, is your first lesson on how tempting works. It is two-fold. First, the role of a tempter is an important one, for we are vital to combat threats against our kind. As tempters, we can peer into the depths of anyone's mind and influence their decisions. We are masters of deception and persuasion. To achieve this, we must engage our subject's senses." The class remains silent, absorbing her words.

"While you are new to your abilities, it may be beneficial for you to use eye contact as a means of facilitating your deception. The only limit to your Offering is found in your dedication to mastering it. It may come easy for some, while others may have to work relentlessly at it. And second, don't cause disruptions in my class and expect there to be no consequences!"

"Did you hear that, Jane?" Duplicity asks, glaring at me. "We can peer into the depths of anyone's mind...maybe soon you can find out who your father is." The class giggles at her remark. *EX-CUSE ME?!* I feel the sudden heat of blood rushing to my face. My jaw clenches as I return my gaze to the Fairmaster without a word. *There goes my hope she will bully someone else this year.*

"To continue," the Fairmaster raises her voice, "You may call me Fairmaster Beguile. And although I am here to teach you the ways of a tempter, it is also important for you to understand the other Offerings. Who can tell me what our conditioners control?"

"The weather and elements," a short boy in front says.

"Correct. Growers?"

"They create and cultivate all plant life," he says.

The Fairmaster questions him even further, "And how much of the future can a foreseer observe?" The boy is silent, thinking as we all await his answer. *Poor guy*. His face reddens and he shakes his head in uncertainty.

Duplicity rolls her eyes. "They only see what affects their own future," she scoffs, all but labeling the boy an idiot.

The Fairmaster nods. "True, but just like with tempting, the success of any student is attributed to hard work. Some have been known to see the futures of others. The foreseers who discern which Offering each of us carries inside, for example, even while it lies in wait."

"Can they see everything that will happen? And how many of them are that strong?" the girl next to me shouts.

"No. They can't see everything, only glimpses so far as I understand it. And I only know of six that are..." Fairmaster Beguile looks away uncomfortably, "alive today." I stare down at my boots, sensing all eyes on me. *Next subject, please!* She clears her throat. "Now, here's a tough one. Is there anything on this green earth that healers are unable to heal?"

"No!" the short boy responds, excited to know another answer.

The Fairmaster folds her arms with a teasing smile. "Incorrect. Healers can restore everything, *except* a broken heart. So, in my class, you will focus on your schoolwork and not your cute classmates." She chuckles to herself before continuing, "Today we will begin our practice with animals." She walks toward the open window and squints out. "Aha! Perfect," she says, pointing at one of the branches. "Come closer. Take a look."

I scoot closer and strain my eyes. A small, nearly invisible chameleon clings to a branch, camouflaging himself against it. The Fairmaster locks her gaze and extends her hand out. The chameleon inches closer until it climbs into her palm. "Duplicity, what is your favorite color?" she asks, turning to face us with the chameleon in hand.

Duplicity shoots me another threatening glance. "Blood red."

The brown pigmentation of the chameleon's scales blush to a violent red instantaneously. A few people in front of me gasp. They must not know many tempters. Or avoid them like I do. That's a petty party trick as temptings usually go. "Alright, let's settle back down now that we've had a little fun. Everyone, please find a seat," Fairmaster Beguile says after releasing the chameleon outside.

I make a dash for the desk in the back right corner. It's close to a window and I'm hoping being in the back of the room will spare me from being called on often. Spiderwebs hang from the legs of the chair. I shudder, then kick them down with my boot and take a seat. Someone carved the name "Hoax" into the top left corner of my desk. A used quill and jar of ink wait for me in the center.

Most of the school day is spent with the Fairmaster leading the typical icebreakers and introductions. I stare out the window in a daze until it comes time for me to rise and introduce myself. As I lumber to my feet, Fairmaster Beguile says, "Before you begin, I'd like to offer you my condolences. Sibyl was a…" she pauses, trying to find the right words, "…*unique* woman."

"Thank you," I squeak. I assumed word would spread quickly of Mother's death, but the awkward silence in the class confirms it. Everyone knows. The death of a former Elder, even a disgraced one, is still newsworthy.

"But keep in mind, I will not be going easy on any of my students, regardless of what misfortunes they may have throughout the school year. I want all my students to be thoroughly trained masters of tempting, that does not come without rigorous challenges. Now, go ahead and introduce yourself."

I freeze, nervous about what to say as all eyes rest on me. "My name is Jane…and…I'm happy to be here." I slump back into my seat, embarrassed by my cringe-worthy self-introduction. My long brown hair falls forward around my face, and I'm hoping it will be enough to shade me from any wandering stares.

As the day drones on, friends are catching up, and new connections are forming. I try to participate and fake a smile, but my classmates avoid me. I've never had a lot of friends so I'm not expecting much, but I feel so bad that any kind word would be welcomed.

"This evening, I want you to try implementing your power of persuasion on an animal. Remember, eye contact is key for a beginner. Make sure you lock eyes with your selection. Once you have established the connection, impress your will on the animal with your mind. This will take a significant amount of concentration, but it is already within you, so have faith in yourself. That will be all for today," the Fairmaster says.

Everyone jumps from their seats and hustles outside. I follow my peers back onto the deck, but sense someone watching me. A subtle side glance confirms it to be Fairmaster Lily, the growing Fairmaster. *Sheesh. Even the adults won't let me grieve in peace.* I dart for the stairs, but it's congested with students. "Jane!" she calls. I turn around slowly, feigning surprise.

Lily's arms cradle a large wicker basket bursting with fruits and vegetables. "I'm so sorry for the loss of your mother. I didn't know her personally, but she really made a name for herself," she coos. She sets the basket down to reach for my hands and gently clasps them in hers. Something tickles my palms. I part my hands to the shape of a cup and watch the delicate expansion of a white lily atop my fingers. *Okay, now I feel bad.* I force a smile, holding back tears.

"Thank you, Fairmaster Lily. You are so thoughtful," I whisper without meaning to. Lily grins with glossy eyes. She plucks the flower from my hands and tucks the stem behind my ear. Her dainty hands rest on my shoulders to hold me at arm's length. With a reassuring nod, she drapes the strap of the heavy basket across my shoulder and kindly waves me off, turning to catch up with her own students.

In years prior, I would've already smelled juicy pies baking long before my tree was in view. I'd rush up, eager to share the events of the day with Mother. But no such sweet smells welcome me back today. And no one is home to ask me how my first day at the Redwoods went. No one will ask me if others had been kind to me, or if I'd made any new friends. Even the creak of my wooden door sounds sad.

I set the basket down and massage my aching arms. I'm not hungry, but I know I need to put something on my empty stomach. I light a fire in the hearth under the same pot of stew I prepared for myself the night before. The smell of burnt vegetables rises faintly from the pot, and the thought crosses my mind that the soup has long since spoiled. But I don't care.

After forcing down a few bites, I set the bowl aside and replay Mother's last words in my mind. Angry tears roll down my cheeks. *I'm so important! Yeah, right!*

The sound of beating wings jars me from my bout of self-pity. I get up to shoo the pesky bird but remember my assignment. I exhale slowly and focus on his small, beady eyes. The bird hovers for a moment, chirping at me.

"Here, birdy-birdy. Come on, land on my shoulder," I say aloud. Another chirp is all I get. I whistle to coax him closer.

The bird flies toward me. My heart leaps in my chest. He flies lower, and closer, now within arm's reach. He dives right down into my soup, splashing it everywhere. His yellow beak skewers a chunk of potato, and he takes flight. He makes a swift exit, but not before ejecting his previous meal onto the hardwood floor. "I'll stuff my pillow with you!" I scream after the miserable bird, slamming the window shutters closed. I want to rage at the skies, but all I can manage are some quiet tears.

THREE

THE SONGS OF EARLY BIRDS rouse me the following morning. My eyes peek open, adjusting to the rays of sun beaming through my window. I melt out of bed, throw on a clean shirt, and shimmy into the same pants I wore the day before. My stomach growls, but there is no time to make breakfast. I'm late.

I quickly rummage through the basket Lily had given me. I toss a couple of apples into my satchel and head for the door. I twist it open and jump back at the sight of Herald, poised to knock. It is unusual for an Elder to make a house call after a death, but Mother had groomed him to take her place as an Elder. Perhaps he is here out of respect. I can't be sure of his motive.

"Er–Hello, Jane. I was hoping to have a moment of your time t—to…to discuss your mother's affairs," he says.

"I was actually just on my way to school, so now's not a good time," I say, backing him up a step with my hard stare. *You didn't even bother to ask how I'm doing.*

"I see. Of course. You have school. In that case, would it be okay if I stopped by afterward?"

I can tell by his persistent tone that he isn't going to let up. "Sure. I'm sorry—I'm running late so I really must go." I slam the door shut and march past him and down the steps from my tree-house as he follows several paces behind.

Rather annoyed to begin my day meeting his wild eyebrows and chubby cheeks, I pretend not to hear him when he calls after me, "See you this afternoon!"

My class is just straggling in as I claim my spot in the back of the room, hoping to go unnoticed after yesterday's spectacle. "Good morning, class. Take your seats. We have a lot to do today, so let's jump right in. We'll start with last night's assignment. Who would like to describe their interaction with an animal?" Fairmaster Beguile looks around expectantly. Not a single hand rises to the air. Her eyes land on me. "Jane, why don't you go first?"

My face prickles as I rise to my feet. "Um. A bird—"

"Up front, please. Where we can all see you." *Give me a break, here.*

A frown pulls at my lips as I make my way to the front. I fiddle with my hands and exhale hard. "A bird flew into my house last night. So, I stared him down and had him perch on my shoulder…It took a while, but I was eventually successful." The lie trails off to a whisper. I do not like to lie.

"Yeah, right," Duplicity says, disguised in a cough.

I expect the Fairmaster to scold her for the rude comment, but she doesn't. *Guess she's already decided on a favorite.* Instead, her arms cross and she glares at me. She knows the truth, too. She's already verified with the firsthand account from my brain. That story is absolutely false. But she finally looks away without commenting on my fib. Her smile reappears when she asks, "How about you, Duplicity?" as I drag myself back to my seat.

Duplicity flips her bouncy, red hair. "I could tell you…or I could just show you." She then proceeds to strut to the open window in the back, nearest me. I twist around to watch as she kneels by the sill and scours the grounds below. There, sticking out like a sore thumb, a small black and white ball of fur pokes around in the bushes.

She raises her fingers to her lips and lets out an ear-piercing whistle. The skunk jerks around, cocking his head up toward the sound. I'm sure he'll make a run for it. No way Duplicity can hold a connection from that distance. He looks up at the window for only a second.

Duplicity gives a slight nod in the direction of the stairs. The skunk waddles along. *Unbelievable.* Every eye in the room follows him as he circles up the long staircase, coming in and out of our line of sight each time he rounds the trunk. At the top of the deck, he pauses and peers back into Duplicity's gaze. With her hand, she gestures toward a neighboring classroom. He scampers across the bridge and enters the open doorway.

Disgusted cries erupt in unison from the other room. Students flood across the bridge and onto the deck to escape the foul smell. The stench of skunk can linger for days. Our class roars with laughter until an irritated Fairmaster Lily storms inside, holding the skunk by its nape. Duplicity's reputation for teenage antics is well known, so it comes as no surprise when Fairmaster Lily marches straight toward her. She plops the spooked skunk on top of Duplicity's desk saying, "You wouldn't happen to know anything about this, *dear*, would you?"

"I was just practicing my tempting on a skunk, and he got away from me. The little vermin must have gotten scared. I didn't mean any harm, honest," Duplicity answers, accompanied by her most convincing smile.

"Let's agree that it won't happen again, shall we?" Fairmaster Lily waves her hands gracefully around the skunk and hardened vines spring forth out of thin air. They fold on themselves, weaving a primitive cage to trap the creature. "Am I clear?"

Duplicity's smile recoils into a hard line and she nods. Fairmaster Lily pivots sharply and marches back out, leaving the skunk cage on the desk. "Let's all settle down now, class," Fairmaster Beguile says. She walks down the aisle toward Duplicity's desk, picks up the cage, and winks. "Excellent work."

"Thank you, Fairmaster," Duplicity says, grinning widely.

Fairmaster Beguile holds the cage up at eye level and stares directly into the skunk's eyes. *"Now, don't let me catch you in here again."* She opens the cage, places him on the ground, and scoots him toward the door with her boot before he takes off, out of the classroom.

A few more students share their animal experiences before Fairmaster Beguile redirects us. "Students, today we will explore our lands to show how we are all intertwined. Each Offering plays an important role in creating a harmonious environment for us. It takes everyone to make this delicate system work. We'll also be seeing the newborns in this month's Revealing Ceremony, where foreseers will announce their future Offerings. Our first stop will be the Gardens."

We follow the Fairmaster in a single file line back down to the ground. The other classes have already gone on ahead of us. I trail even further behind. I am far enough back to only hear the periodic chirps of birds. Ferns grow lush, lining the sunshine-speckled path. I inhale deeply, smelling the richness of the earth as the crisp air cools my lungs.

After a short hike, I see the familiar-yet-ever-changing super-abundant Gardens, where the community harvest is grown and collected. All varieties of fruits and vegetables stretch across the acreage. Currently framing the Gardens are alternating dogwood and cherry blossom trees in full bloom, painting a beautiful picture of nature's lavish bounty.

A few large houses of oak stand in the back of the Gardens. Their long branches extend far over the grounds creating a canopy for the free market, which I visit often. These homes belong to the primary grower, conditioner, and healer who help maintain the Gardens.

As we gather around the bases of the oaks, a grower lowers himself using a thick vine constructed into a pulley system. He is shirtless and strapping with a golden tan from summer. "Greetings students, my name is Spruce. Welcome to the Gardens where we tend to all of our vegetation," he exclaims. "The conditioners maintain a perfect environment for cultivating all varieties of vegetation, even those not indigenous to this area. Growers, like me, call forth all the plants we use and bring them to life, and our healers prevent crop failure. Now, go and explore!" he says with a toothy grin.

The classes split off into cliques, but I keep to myself…Not as if it's by choice. I watch as a woman walks down a nearby aisle of freshly tilled soil and extends her arms up from her sides. Green seedlings spring up from the earth with each step she takes.

As she toils along the rows, she comes to a patch of tomatoes with small bites missing from the hanging fruit. She motions to a man who kneels closely to observe them. He cradles a tomato in his hands, and the fruit becomes whole again. The man looks over to see me eyeing him and smiles. He plucks the restored tomato from the vine and tosses it to me, before turning back to tend to the rest of the patch.

I take a bite from the plump fruit and meander down to the rows of cornstalks. Nearby giggles snap my head to the left. I gently poke my head through the stalks to get a better look. Augur, a foreseer I only know by name, has Duplicity wrapped in a tight embrace. They are nearly hidden among the tall stalks. I can't help but gawk as Duplicity playfully kisses him and runs her fingers through his short, blond curls.

She catches my gaze and releases him. "Enjoying the show, Jane? If your Offering ever does come in, you can tempt someone to kiss you. Otherwise, you're probably out of luck." She gives Augur a light shove. "You should have seen her coming. You need to work on that." He scoffs and pulls her deeper into the cornfield, away from my prying eyes. *Yikes. What can he possibly see in her?*

"Alright, class, on we go. We have a lot of ground to cover," Fairmaster Beguile calls loudly. I hurry out of the cornstalks to re-join my class. As we're leaving, I spot a woman on the other side of the field. With her arms extended high, she creates a cascade of water over the Gardens. The sun beams through the clear streams of water, glimmering into every color of the rainbow. The system truly is flawless, or so it seems.

FOUR

I KEEP AN EYE ON Duplicity as she hugs Augur goodbye and sinks to the back of the drove closer to me with Ruse, another girl from our class. Duplicity feigns a yawn. "What a snooze fest," she says. Ruse giggles with a swift flip of her black, curly locks. The sun glistens on her ebony skin as she fakes nodding off too but snoring for added effect. I ignore them, hoping I don't alert them to my presence.

Fairmaster Beguile ushers us back into the forest, to journey toward the center of our lands, where the Elders conduct their formal business at the Sanctuary. My heart throbs in my chest as we draw closer to it. I have not seen it for many years. Mother always made excuses for using routes to avoid it, even if that meant going out of our way.

When the Sanctuary finally comes into view, it is just as I remember. It wraps around a very old and gnarled redwood tree and has a wide staircase that leads up to a large balcony. "The Elders are the most powerful individuals from each Offering that keep us protected and thriving," Fairmaster Beguile says as we surround the base of the gigantic tree, craning our necks to look up at the structure. "If any of you are ever fortunate enough to step inside again, you will have reached the pinnacle of power."

After we all reach the balcony, we stop to stare at a set of wooden double doors. Ruse huffs impatiently and reaches her hand out for one of the doorknobs.

"Stop! Are you stupid? Don't you know what those are?" Duplicity shrieks.

"Doorknobs?" Ruse asks, holding up her arms in confusion. The smooth, dark knobs twinkle in the sunlight.

"*Sapphire* doorknobs. They're charged, of course, with the conditioning Offering," Duplicity says, shaking her head like that should have been obvious. I'll admit that I didn't notice either.

"I'm afraid Duplicity is right," Fairmaster Beguile says. "You wouldn't want to touch one of those, that's for sure. Who knows what nasty little trick is waiting to teach your hand a lesson in restraint?" The Fairmaster lifts her right hand above her forehead to block the sun from her eyes and looks out into the distance. Her brow furrows and she mutters, "Now, where might that indolent fool be? He's supposed to be here by now."

The wooden doors swing open. "I hope you haven't been waiting long. The patrolman was supposed to escort you in," Ginger says, her green cloak rippling with her movement.

I hear a faint whistling of the wind and suddenly a puffy cloud whooshes past me. A handsome young man joins us on the balcony as the cloud dissipates beneath his feet. A conditioner. The contrast between his strikingly blue eyes against his dark brown hair is something you cannot miss. He makes a face and shrugs. "Sorry I'm late."

"Don't make it a habit," Ginger mutters, beckoning us all inside.

"Better late than never, Storm," Duplicity says with an eye roll as she skirts past him. He bites his bottom lip, clearly wanting to fire back but stopping himself. I am the last to poke my head inside. It's dim and airless. "Gross. It smells like mildew," Duplicity complains.

As the other students fan out further inside, I scoot in behind everyone. In the center of the room is a large mahogany table surrounded by long benches. Scraps and scrolls of parchment are strewn over the table in a haphazard fashion. Countless volumes of old leather-bound texts line the walls on either side. A large band of drawers covers the back wall, stretching from floor to ceiling. "This place is a mess," Ruse spits.

Students flood Ginger with all manner of questions like: "Where are the other Elders?" and "Which Elder is the most powerful?" while Fairmaster Beguile turns away to scold Ruse for her discourteous comment.

Out of the corner of my eye, I notice Duplicity sneaking toward the old books. I watch her rummage through the drawers and jumbled files, eventually pulling out an especially old wad of parchment. She unfolds it and whispers the prophecy aloud, "Ooh. This one is from Sibyl. 4-1-2-S-E…"

My cheeks burn as I snatch the parchment from her hands. "Let me see that!" I inspect the note closely, memorizing every stroke of the ink:

412 SE Tibbetts St.
Cougar, WA 98616
— Sibyl

Definitely her handwriting. But what could it mean? Duplicity yanks the prophecy away from me. "Jane's crazy mother and her gibberish. What are these random numbers and letters supposed to even mean? I swear, that old *fairy* just made stuff up," she laughs. She shoves the scrap of parchment back into the drawer and slams it shut.

My mouth hangs open. I have only heard the word once or twice in my entire life. A slur of that kind is never thrown around lightly. "You know what, Duplicity?" I say, my heart racing, "Go ahead. Make fun of me all you want. But leave my mother out of it!" Without thinking, I grab a small rock off the table and hurl it at her. What happens next is very different from what I had expected. The room instantly shifts into a windstorm of significant magnitude. The gemstone lands on the floor, discharging a constant surge of wind. The papers on the desk take flight, swirling about the room in a circular motion. *Oops. This is bad.*

I am the first student forcefully pinned to the wall. Duplicity and Ruse drive their heels into the wooden planks of the floor. Their hair swarms over their faces as they attempt to move toward the stone with outstretched hands, but the air current is too strong. Their feet slide backward until they are thrust against the wall next to me. One by one, we all end up trapped and helpless.

"Way to go, Jane!" Duplicity screams over the howls of wind. Of course, that makes me even angrier.

As the airstream continues to whip, a piece of parchment gets stuck to Ruse's face. She pulls it down and glances at it. "Look at this," she shouts, holding up an amateur drawing of the Sanctuary engulfed in flames. The wind hums and moans while the flurry of papers continues to rustle around us.

"STORM! SHUT THAT STONE OFF!" Duplicity's command cuts through the windblast and pierces into Storm like a sharp hook. He hastens his steps, strolling toward the stone with an ease only a conditioner could manage. He picks up the sapphire and rubs it gently, returning the room to its former stuffiness.

"Why, thank you, Storm. That was quite an ordeal," Ginger says, smoothing her hair. She turns to the Fairmaster and adds, "We should wrap this up before Artifice returns from his rounds. Schoolchildren running amuck is sure to send him over the edge, especially here. And that's the last thing I need." The Fairmaster nods, sweeping her long bangs out of her eyes.

Storm blinks repeatedly until his face relaxes and his expression returns. His angry eyes flash at Duplicity. "I would've done that if you could have waited a minute," he hisses, bending over to pick up the loose papers off the floor.

Duplicity smirks as she peels herself from the wall. "You took too long. Nobody likes windblown hair." She stomps out of the Sanctuary with the rest of us rushing out behind her.

"Pretty impressive, tempting him without eye contact. You're getting stronger," Fairmaster Beguile says when she catches up to Duplicity.

"You haven't seen anything yet," Duplicity replies.

"I daresay I believe you. As for you, Jane," Fairmaster Beguile points at me, "do try to stay out of trouble next time." After patting her hair back into place, she clears her throat and roars, "The final stop on our tour will be to witness the Revealing Ceremony. Each of the infants will be placed into one of our five Offerings, based on visions the foreseers receive."

We follow the Fairmaster to an open meadow where several other Fairkind gather around a single moss-covered dwelling. The tree is shared by three of the oldest and wisest foreseers. Candles decorate the front and rows of tree stumps seat the crowd.

The foreseers emerge from the house, and all fall silent, except for the soft coos of infants. They descend one by one down the steps, dressed in formal silver cloaks similar to Herald's. Each of the three—Presage, Prophet, and Omen—bears a striking resemblance. The many years they've spent together seem to have morphed them into one.

Omen raises a bony hand to beckon the first Fairkind couple and their newborn. The mother cradles the child, while each of the three places a pointer finger on the infant's forehead and closes their eyes. They reopen them and exchange whispers. "This child shall be a grower. What name will you give her?" Prophet roars, his voice carrying throughout the area.

"Rosemary!" the parents exclaim. Applause fills the clearing as the couple takes their infant and rejoins the crowd. One by one, the infants are named according to their future Offerings. Witnessing it for the first time makes me wonder what the foreseers saw in my future when I was a baby. And why Mother settled on the peculiar name of Jane, instead of something more fitting and traditional.

When the ceremony concludes, I sprint after the three foreseers. Out of breath, I tap the one in the middle on the shoulder from behind. "Hello, I don't know if you remember me—"

"Hello, Jane," Omen turns around to cut me off. "You are wondering why we placed you as a tempter, yes?"

"Nothing gets past a foreseer." I laugh nervously. The three men stare at me without blinking.

"We deliberated for a long time. But a vision came to me of a cougar pursuing you. You were able to deceive it into no longer seeing you, yet you remained in front of the beast all the while. Give it time, Jane," Omen croaks.

My eyes widen, horrified. *Yikes.* "I see…and do you happen to know why my mother named me Jane? I never asked her because I didn't want her to think I disliked what she had chosen. It's just so different is all."

"It perplexed me also. But Sibyl always had a mind of her own. And it is only a name," he answers. He and the others turn to leave.

"Wait—"

Omen stops in his tracks and turns back around slowly while Presage and Prophet proceed on to their house of oak. A tinge of sadness hangs in his knowing eyes. "I'm sorry, Jane. It was only Sibyl at your ceremony. I haven't the faintest idea who your father is."

"I knew it was a long shot. Thanks anyway."

FIVE

WITH A SPRING IN MY step, I bounce home. I still don't know who my father is, but I figure things will start to look up after my conversation with Omen. My time will come to show my Offering. That is enough to spark a little hope. My mood plummets when I see a hunched, cloaked figure pacing my balcony.

Herald is waiting for my return, just as he'd said he would be. His brazen tuft, protruding like a flag at full mast, is unmistakable from any distance. I grimace at the sight of it.

I huff up the stairs, hoping that my unwelcoming demeanor will be enough to keep the conversation to a minimum. "Jane, hello again. How are you?" His tone is sympathetic, more tactful than earlier.

"I'm fine, thanks," I mutter. "So, what can I do for you?"

"I hate to be a bother, but I'm here to collect any extra recorded visions that Sibyl may have been keeping," he says with shifty eyes, not meeting mine.

"I haven't gone through her things yet, but I'm not aware of any. I never saw her write anything down as far back as I can remember. Maybe once or twice when I was younger. What is this all about, anyway? What exactly are you looking for?"

"Frankly, we suspect your mother may have been hiding things from us, and it is imperative that we know what, and more importantly, why."

"Sure. I have nothing to hide," I say curtly. "But you better find some proof if you're going to throw around accusations like that." I step aside to let him through and lead the way into Mother's room. I gesture to a wooden desk I seldom saw her use. "I'm guessing if she had any visions that she recorded, they'd be in there."

Herald looks down at some drawings on the desk with a puzzled stare. "What's all this?"

I lean into my left heel and fold my arms. "She was cooped up in her room for nearly a year. She liked to paint. Big deal."

"...She never talked about them? The—the people...with wings?"

"Nope. She never talked about her doodles with me." He doesn't look at me, analyzing the silly paintings a moment longer before laying them back down. He eyes a bookstack with an old painter's palette on top. The paint is dry and cracked. Dirty brushes dangle precariously on top with hardened bristles. I watch Herald, practically breathing down his neck, as he picks up each of the books and combs through them. Frantically, he searches for something, anything.

He yanks open a slim drawer that holds a few quills and bottles of ink. The brilliance of a stone catches my eye, one I had forgotten existed. Mother's gold-encrusted diamond brooch flashes from the depths of the drawer. Apart from the grime, it looks identical to the one pinned on Herald's left breast of his cloak. It is the mark of an Elder to don the stone of their Offering.

According to tradition, tempters wear rubies which embody their seductive nature. Foreseers wear diamonds to represent the clarity of their visions and ability to see through to the future. Emeralds are chosen for the growers as they match the lush green of the flora they create. Opals are a symbol of healers because the sparkle from the stone symbolizes their ability to bring someone back from death's clutches. Conditioners wear sapphires, like a dark blue sky drizzling down on the rainiest of days. And such is the accepted belief of the origin of the Elders' stones for as long as anyone can remember.

Herald's stone is polished and shining, looking a bit ostentatious against his pristine silver cloak. He picks up Mother's brooch and looks it over. It's clear he too has not seen it in ages. "Well, would you look at that?" he mutters under his breath.

"I'll take that," I snap, snatching it from his hand.

Herald frowns. "It's regrettable how things turned out for Sibyl."

"Don't you have any compassion? None of you ever cared about her. I can see that now." *I am being rude, but I am also angry.*

Herald continues his search in silence. He carelessly tosses papers and books everywhere, too preoccupied for a rebuttal. I fold my arms across my chest and raise an eyebrow in defiance. "Do you have to make such a mess? And shouldn't you already know what you're looking for and where to find it if there were anything?" *Some foreseer you are.*

Most people have figured out by now that the only reason Herald was a suitable replacement for Mother is because he was single. I once heard Mother credit his lack of a spouse to his unsightly appearance and off-putting personality. I've only met the man a handful of times, but I'd say she was on to something. I raise my voice, "I'm going to have to ask you to leave if you won't give me some answers."

Herald stands up straight and adjusts the collar of his cloak. He sighs deeply, looking pressed for time. "Honestly? We've never seen a more powerful foreseer than your mother and—I probably shouldn't be telling you this—but before your mother was pregnant with you, she prophesied a great danger to the Fairkind. If her proclamation is correct, that threat would rise to power sometime soon. It's my duty to get to the bottom of it."

"Has anyone else seen this danger? Have you?"

"No. Not as of yet."

"And who's to say the future hasn't changed? That was a long time ago."

"We've considered that, and perhaps it has. But if the safety of our kind is at stake, it's worth a little investigating." He resumes his snooping, exiting Mother's room, and bringing his search to the other parts of the house. His nose scrunches as he enters the kitchen. The old pot of vegetable soup still hangs in the hearth, only now it reeks putrid. A sudden pang of embarrassment hits me.

Herald glances at the rotting pot and catches a glimpse of something else in the hearth, something I had failed to see. He squints for a moment, leaning closer. He reaches his hand in for it and brushes away the dried cinders and ash. It is a very small, very tattered, burnt piece of parchment. "What is this?" he asks, angling it for me to have a look.

I inspect the paper carefully. Only one word is written on it, repeatedly. *Kismet.* "I've never seen this before. I have no idea what it means or where it came from."

"It's your mother's handwriting, is it not?"

Yes. "It looks like it, but it's just gibberish."

Herald's brow furrows. "I don't think it's gibberish. I think it means something."

"Good. I'm glad you found what you were looking for. If there isn't anything else I can do for you, I really need to focus on my studies."

Herald makes a face but reluctantly obliges me. He turns to leave, paper still clenched in his hand. Once outside, he turns back to add, "If you find anything else—"

"I know where to find you," I say and firmly close the door. I spy on him from the window as he leaves. He trots along the path away from my house, making haste deeper into the wood. I suck in a sharp breath as Artifice steps out of the shadows. Herald hands him the note. Artifice reads it and then crumples it in his fist, glancing straight up to my window. I duck out of sight, hoping he didn't see me.

I sit there on the floor for a while after that, turning Mother's old brooch over in my hands. *Maybe she was hiding something—something big.*

SIX

I REMAIN CROUCHED BENEATH THE window, only my eyes breaching the sill. Artifice and Herald loiter a moment or two longer but soon vanish from my line of sight. After returning Mother's brooch to her writing desk, I drag myself into the kitchen. I heave the pot of muck out of the hearth and pinch my nose with my free hand. The stench still manages to soar up my snout and I gag.

I dump the pot outside and return upstairs to examine the hearth in private, curious to see if any other messages are hiding inside. Nope. Herald's visit has left me more puzzled than ever. I need to clear my head. Mother would encourage me to practice my tempting. Or would she? I'm not so sure anymore. After a few minutes of silent pacing, I light a torch and head out into the dusk. My feet have other plans for me.

I can feel the erratic thumping of my heart as I enter the Tavern for the first time. The old, stony cave is on the outskirts of our community. There is no age requirement, but the crowd of regulars does not typically consist of young schoolgirls. If Mother were alive, going on a school night would be out of the question. Any other night, too, for that matter.

It's very loud, with boisterous men gulping down their pints in clusters. They are utterly oblivious of the strategically deployed ladies, batting their eyes to be noticed. Long streams of wax drip from wooden candelabras in the center of each table, not one of which hosts an empty chair. My eyes do a quick sweep of the room, spotting only one vacant seat—a stool at the bar. I hang my torch next to the others that line the wall and make a beeline for it.

Each end of the bar is punctuated by heavily fruited citrus trees. Mint and other herbs dangle from cracks in the cave's ceiling. I take a seat and glance at the man next to me. It's the same conditioner from earlier at the Sanctuary. *What did Duplicity say his name was? Oh, right—Storm.*

He has just the right amount of stubble and sloppy tresses which fall in waves above his carefully chiseled chin. Our eyes lock briefly before I look away. "What are you drinking?" I hear him ask. My heart skips a beat as I slowly glance back at his face. His eyes are fixed on me, confirming my fear. I was the intended target of his question.

I try to respond, but I'm suddenly so nervous, I just smile and shrug. I'll admit, I'm not that great at casual interactions. He flags down a bartender buzzing behind the counter and orders, "Two mint muddles, please, and put them on me."

The woman shakes her head. "You still owe me from last time, Storm. I've been waiting awhile for you to pressure-wash my tree."

"Come on, I'll swing by this weekend…I'll even burn the brush around your yard."

"Fine. You got yourself a deal," she says. She looks me over once and flashes him a not-so-subtle wink before darting off.

He leans into my ear and my entire body tenses. "You'll have to excuse Blossom. She takes sick pleasure in making me uncomfortable—especially around females. I'm Storm." He gently rubs his hand over his heart and extends it out to me, which takes me by surprise. It is a formal greeting for a proper first encounter, one that I've always found endearing but rarely had the opportunity to use. People tend to avoid such courtesies when it comes to me. The illegitimate outcast.

The cave lighting is dim which I appreciate. I don't want him to see the blush on my cheeks. I rub my hand in a circular motion above my heart and tenderly slide into his grip. The unexpected warmth of his skin practically invites me to stroke the backside of his hand with my thumb, but I yank my hand back before I can do anything so creepy. "Good to meet you, Storm. I'm Jane," I finally manage to say. "What was all that about?"

"With Blossom?" he asks. I nod. "That's kind of how this place works. The bartenders have their regular work posts during the day and volunteer here at night."

"Why would they work extra?" I ask. *That sounds exhausting.*

"They rack up favors from people with different Offerings. They also accept gemstones, but those are hard to come by."

Blossom returns with two mugs. "I haven't seen you in here before," she says. "What brings a young lady, such as yourself, this way?" The dangling mint stretches down from the ceiling to meet her hands. But her eyes stay on me, waiting for my response.

"I've had a rough couple of days," I say grimly.

She laughs and plucks a few sprigs. "Everyone in here's had a rough couple of days. When you can string enough bad days together, consider yourself a regular." The mint quickly recoils back up to the ceiling. She holds the leaves in her left palm and abruptly slaps them with her right hand.

"What are you doing?" I ask in bewilderment.

"It brings out the flavor of the mint. Don't worry, you'll love it," she says with another slap. She drops a few leaves into each of the mugs and shoots her hand out above my head. Down plunges a freshly snapped ginger root into her palm. I duck instinctively but my reflexes are admittedly slow. She's already peeled the ginger and tossed it into the mugs before I can straighten my back out.

She sweeps her gaze now and then, keeping an eye out for her next thirsty customer. "Be right with you!" she says, flashing her flirty smile to one of her regulars. She muddles our drinks with a wooden pestle and pours fermented nectar over the mint and ginger. A dash of honey tops them off. After a quick swirl, she slips a lime wedge on each rim and slides them out to Storm and me.

"Thank you," I say, reaching for my mug.

Storm holds his hand up. "Wait." He grasps both mugs and holds them tightly in his grip until they exhale an icy, cool vapor. "It's better chilled," he says with a wink.

"Good idea."

"So...Jane...That's an interesting name—what Offering?"

"Tempting." I take a sip of my drink. The strength hits me like a fist to the face and I automatically cough.

He studies me curiously. "No offense...but you don't seem like the tempting type."

"I'll take that as a compliment," I say, tossing my hair playfully.

"Oh?"

"I hate my class at the Redwoods. Well, one girl in particular—you know her actually—Duplicity."

Storm chuckles, revealing his winsome smile. "Ah, yes. Unfortunately, I do."

"Go on..."

"Believe it or not, she's my ex-girlfriend. We broke up over the summer. Left me for some foreseer kid."

"It's nice to meet another victim," I say. He raises his mug and clinks it against mine. "I already have enough on my plate without her drama. My mother just died. I can't seem to figure out how to use my Offering. The last thing I need is some attention-crazed bully." I hang my head and catch myself subconsciously counting the dozens of water rings permanently stained on the wooden bar. My bottom lip curves forward only for a second before I bite it. I refuse to let myself pout. *I'm too old for that.* I peek back up at Storm to measure his reaction to what I've just realized were unsolicited admissions.

His tone is kind saying, "You must be Sibyl's daughter. I'm sorry for your loss."

"You knew her?"

"Everyone knew her...or about her, at least." I roll my eyes without thinking. "Hey—I didn't mean it like that..."

"Sorry...that wasn't directed at you. It's not your fault every-one gossips about her." I let out a long sigh. "I really miss her."

He pats me a little too hard on the shoulder and I flinch. We sit there for a few moments, sipping our drinks in silence. After I finish mine, I swirl my mug around the damp surface of the bar. The obnoxious clinking of ice perpetuates the tension. My face lights up when Blossom returns to break the silence. "Another roun—,"

"Yes, please!" I accidentally cut her off.

"Coming right up," she says and flutters off again.

Storm raises an eyebrow, hinging the left side of his lip into a smirk. "Aren't you a little lush?"

My forehead pinches in confusion. "Is that bad?"

"No, I'm kidding. Unless you are, in fact, an alcoholic?"

"Oh, no. This is my first time."

"You better take it easy. This stuff will hit you fast and hard." Blossom returns with our next round, and I gulp mine down despite Storm's warning. Each additional round tastes even sweeter than the one before. Soon, I am dizzy and too sozzled to stand.

"I need to be going...dome. I mean home. I'm leaving," I say, feeling strange.

Storm holds his hands out to steady me. "Do you need an escort?"

"No, no. Thanks. I'll be fine...I'm just tired."

"That's smart. You should sleep it off." I wobble somewhat to the exit, barely making it outside before falling flat on my face. I pick myself up and skip along, turning this way and that until I come to a fork in the trail. I teeter a moment. I know the way home. I've been this way a thousand times, but everything is wrong. My head spins. The two trails morph into three and four, and then back to two.

I veer left and waddle along the path until it disappears into thick forest. Pushing through the unfamiliar brush, I see the faint glimmer of water under the pale moonlight. I stagger onto the bank of a secluded lagoon and steady myself against a large rock to take off my boots. The sand is cold and gritty, squishing between my toes.

I creep down to the water's edge. The calm, glossy surface begs to be shattered. I dip a toe in, sending ripples across the slick surface. The temperature is a perfect lukewarm.

I slide off my shirt and trousers, toss them next to my boots, and wade into the lagoon. When my feet can no longer touch the bottom, I take a deep breath and sink beneath the surface. My grief momentarily rolls away with the slight waves, lapping the shore. After a few somersaults, I pop back up for air and tread water.

I paddle out to the middle and flip onto my back, floating under the canopy of stars. The night sky is clear, and they are all visible. I lie on the bed of water for what seems like hours, gazing at the constellations.

Finally noticing the late hour, I abandon my floating position to discover the water level has fallen well below my shoulders. It is sinking. Fast. Fear creeps up my spine as I speed-swim back toward the bank. With each stroke, the shore races toward me like a receding tide until I find myself face down in the soggy, wet sand. A few wide-eyed trout flop beside me. The lagoon is gone.

I jump to my feet, still bare, and squint into the woods. It's useless. I can't see anything in the pitch-black. The bushes rustle behind me, and I jerk my head over my shoulder. "Is someone there?" I call into the darkness. Silence. The hairs on the back of my neck stand on end and I shiver. I cover my privates and bolt for my clothes.

A silhouette emerges from the shadows, tall and masculine. When he steps into a gleam of moonlight, I can make out the details of his face. I don't know him but remember seeing him in passing at the Tavern. "Stop! Don't come any closer!" I stammer, wrestling to yank my clothes over my wet body.

"Forgive me. I was just making my way home and came to see what all the splashing was about," he says with a sly smile. His bloodshot eyes flicker.

"Pervert!"

He shrugs and lifts his left hand toward the empty lagoon. With a swift, downward motion he drops his arm back toward the ground. The collection of moisture in the air condenses and gushes back into the lagoon with a loud crash. The water rolls out in angry waves.

"You seem sober enough to make your way home now, so I'll be on my way. But I'll have to remember to come back here—some real beautiful views this time of night," he says, biting his lip seductively. "My name is Ash, by the way—not pervert," he adds before slinking back into the woods.

SEVEN

I AM THE FIRST TO bustle out of class the next day, racing across the wobbly bridge. My eyes fix on the shaky planks until I crash my skull into another student's. I let out a sharp moan, grazing my throbbing right temple.

"Oh, I'm so sorry. That was all my fault," the bubbly blond says as I step onto the landing. Her big brown eyes shine with kindness as she reaches out and gently strokes the side of my face. "I'm such a klutz. Are you injured? Do you feel any pain? I can heal you, you know," she rattles off.

"No, that's okay. I'm fine. I wasn't paying attention."

"I'm Remedy, pleased to meet you." The pretty girl rubs her palm over her heart and holds out a delicate hand. *Twice in two days. This must be some kind of record.* Her hand is still outstretched, and she makes a face.

"And I'm Jane," I quickly mimic the gesture and clasp her hand. "Sorry to leave you hanging."

"That's quite alright," she says with a warm smile. Something about this quirky girl's presence sparks a smile to cross my lips, too. "Maybe I'll see you at the cliffs tonight?" Remedy's soft curls bounce along to the tune of her sweet voice.

"What's happening at the cliffs?"

"You know…the tradition. Last year's graduates help us use our Offerings. Didn't anyone tell you in class?"

"No…"

"You're welcome to come."

"Well, I –"

She places her gentle hand on my shoulder. "It will be fun. Just think about it," she says, smiling encouragingly. "I'd better be going. We're meeting at sunset. I hope to see you there." I nod and watch her prance away. Truthfully, I'm in no position to decline a potential new friend.

The cliffs are on the other side of the forest, so I sprint to make it there before sundown. I slow my pace once I reach the top, right before they drop off into the ocean. A bunch of students are already mingling, nearly screaming over the deafening crashes of waves against the rocks below.

Surprisingly, Storm is the first face I recognize. He shoots me a half-smile and waves his hand. I return the wave and search the crowd for Remedy. When I find her, her eyes light up. "Jane, I'm so glad you came!"

"I've been meaning to get out more. Thanks for inviting me."

"It looks like the boys are already fired up," she says, pointing to some healer boys from her class.

One of them bends down abruptly to crawl on all fours, pacing like a wolf. After padding around like so, he perches himself on the edge of the cliff and howls at the rising moon. Remedy and I can't help but giggle at the bizarre scene. Another boy shakes his shoulders saying, "Quit gawking at the tempter girls. We've got work to do." The wolf-boy shakes his head a couple of times to snap himself from the daze.

"Keep your eyes to yourself! Or, next time, I'll have you thinking you're a dung beetle!" Ruse yells.

The flustered male rises to his feet, shooting her a nasty look. He turns back to his friends and shouts, "Back to work! It's my turn! Punch me already!" His disheveled hair parts over his forehead, exposing his bulging vein.

His buddy leans back and socks him with a right hook, clean across the jaw. A white fragment flies from his mouth. "My tooth!" he wails, blood spraying with the words. The boy winces, gently rubbing his hand over the injury. After a few minutes of caressing his face, the blood vanishes, and the swelling reverses. His wounds are gone. He smiles big, not a tooth out of place. The other boys square up, striking each other and timing how long it takes for them to heal themselves. They make a game of the violence.

We roll our eyes and turn our sights to a group of six growers standing around the jutted edge of the cliff, peering down at the unfriendly sea below. They back up slowly and grasp hands. With a running leap, they dive off the cliff and out of sight.

We run closer, along with a few others who witnessed the plunge. Suddenly, the ground rumbles and shakes and I lose my footing. Remedy pulls me away from the edge right before an enormous root explodes through the earth, twisting wildly. Then another appears. And another. And another. And another. Growing thicker and longer into sturdy vines as they shoot out from the ground. They curl over the cliff's edge and race down after the jumpers.

Remedy sees it before I do. But the panic in her eyes is urgent enough to help me put two and two together. *Oh no!* Only five vines race down the side of the cliff, and six growers are currently free-falling toward the rocky waters below. One by one the slack pulls taut, and the vines jerk to a stop. They slowly retract back into the earth and four growers heave onto the refuge of the cliff by their makeshift bungees.

The fifth vine retracts much slower. A trim girl with black hair and almond eyes finally drags up onto the cliffside. I know her. Kind of. Belladonna is nice to everyone, even me. Once safely afoot, Belladonna hoists up her vine. "Just hold on tight! I've got you!" she shouts over the cliff. She grunts as she muscles up the remainder of the vine.

A pale hand finally reaches up to grab the edge. I breathe out a hard sigh as the young man rolls onto the cliffside to catch his breath. "That almost ended badly," Remedy says.

"You're telling me! Thanks for having my back."

"I would say anytime but hopefully exploding roots are sort of a one-and-done thing." A smile crosses her face, and we share a quick laugh.

I nudge her. "Shh. Here comes trouble," I whisper and nod toward Duplicity strutting over to Belladonna.

Remedy crosses her arms. "This should be good."

"What are you doing over here with the growers?" Duplicity asks, wrapping her arm around Belladonna's shoulder. "*Such a talented conditioner should be over with the others, showing them how it's done.*"

Belladonna is silent as she walks in sync with Duplicity over to the conditioners, eyes locked. "Just returning one of your stragglers. Belladonna is ready to practice her conditioning." Duplicity winks at Storm.

He shakes his head. "Don't drag me into this."

I'm relieved to see he isn't going to play along. Duplicity rolls her eyes and spots Ash approaching. "Ash, you know Belladonna. She needs help with rain."

"What?" he asks, confused. Duplicity elbows him in his side. "Ouch!"

"Help her make rain!" she demands.

Ash rubs his ribs. "Okay—okay. Hello to you too." He waves his hand in front of Belladonna's blank stare. She doesn't blink.

"Um…just lift your hands to the sky and pull the rain out of the clouds," he says, unsure of himself. Belladonna jerks her arms high above her head. Her eyes fix on the sky, but it remains clear.

"Try fire!" Duplicity yells.

"Okay. Rub your hands together until they feel warm. Then pull them apart to create a ball of fire, like this." He parts his hands and a fiery ball hovers in between them. He takes a deep breath and expels a blast of frigid air, extinguishing the fire. "Your turn."

Belladonna vigorously rubs her hands, then opens them slowly. A bright, red ghost pepper appears in her palms. The sound of Duplicity's callous laughter dispels Belladonna from her trance. "At least you got the *hot* part right," Ash chuckles. Belladonna's eyes flare and she chucks the pepper at his face.

"Relax. It was a joke," Duplicity says.

"You just can't stand when you're not the center of attention, can you?" Belladonna snaps.

"Please. No one cares that you grew a flimsy vine."

Belladonna clenches her fists, eyes burning with rage. "I can do a lot more than that, Duplicity. But I wonder how powerful *you* would be without those pretty green eyes of yours." Belladonna charges Duplicity and tackles her to the ground. She straddles her and smothers her eyes with leaves grown from her palms. "These are poisonous blinding tree leaves, you *fairy!*" she cackles.

"AHH! GET OFF ME!" Duplicity screams. Her eyes seem to triple in size and red splotches dot her face as her skin reacts to the toxins. Duplicity swings her right arm with her eyes ballooned shut. A fresh vine wraps around her wrist, jerking it back down to the ground at her side. She then tries swinging with her left, but Belladonna secures that arm too. *The pain must be blocking Duplicity's concentration from tempting someone without sight.*

Belladonna steps back, towering over Duplicity strapped to the earth. Duplicity wriggles with tearful, bloodshot eyes. "Well, don't just stand there!" she barks blindly at the spectators. Ruse rushes to her side and tries to loosen the vines, but they only tighten.

"You really know how to bring out the worst in people, don't you, Duplicity?" Remedy says.

"HELP ME!" Duplicity yells in the wrong direction.

Remedy scrunches her nose and mouths *"Help me"* and sticks out her tongue. My hand muffles my laughter. She is brave to stand up to her, but she doesn't have to see her every day like I do. After a tad more squirming from Duplicity, Remedy kneels beside her, gently caressing her puffy skin, massaging away the swelling and redness until Duplicity's beauty returns.

"Okay, Belladonna, it was funny. But she's suffered enough. Let her go," Remedy urges. She tugs at the vines still cuffed to Duplicity's wrists. Belladonna grits her teeth. But as Remedy continues to pull, they loosen and fall off. Remedy runs her index finger around the rope burns on Duplicity's wrists until they, too, disappear.

"Next time, I'll make sure it's a permanent impairment," Belladonna warns and walks off.

Ruse pulls Duplicity to her feet. Duplicity shakes out her hair with her fingers and turns to face Remedy. "Hmph. At least your Offering is good for something," she says before storming back to the tempters with Ruse. Remedy rolls her eyes when she's gone.

"Just ignore her. You're a great healer," I say.

"Oh, it was no sweat. But that girl is a monster."

"Yeah. You're lucky you don't have class with her."

EIGHT

I HAVE TRIED TO GET out of bed twice now but have only been able to cock my leg lazily over the side so far. It's becoming increasingly difficult for me to show my face in class given my "abnormality" as Fairmaster Beguile keeps calling it. Several grueling weeks have come and gone, but I remain without my Offering. I hate to be bitter about it, but it seems like an important detail my "all-knowing" mother probably should have mentioned.

I stretch as big as I can and swing both of my feet to the floor. The wooden planks are cold as I press into them. I move like a slug, but get myself dressed, fed, and off to school.

Fairmaster Beguile paces the front with a furrowed brow and anxious eyes. "Quickly, everyone, take your seats. Today we have a very special visitor. Each of our great Elders has set aside today to visit their Offerings to assist all of you young learners in your training. I am humbled to announce our honored guest. Welcome, Artifice!"

Artifice's looming presence enters the classroom several seconds before he does. The sharp edges of his red cloak barely sway as he troops down the aisle to the front. His shiny, black boots squeak with each step. He turns to face us. "Students, I will be the object of your tempting today." He gestures to himself with a terse smile. "Seasoned tempters can resist the tempting of another. Because of this, it is more difficult to establish a connection with a fellow tempter. But I will be making myself vulnerable to allow you all in. Any questions?" No one flinches. "Then let us begin."

"Form a line, students, and don't push. Everyone will get a turn," Fairmaster Beguile says. A lanky boy named Cajole is herded to the front. His legs alone add at least four feet to his body, but it's hard to tell from his slouching. Artifice nods for him to begin, and the boy gulps hard. About a minute ticks past before Artifice squishes his face into a childlike grimace. He lets out a high-pitched, infantile wail and stretches his arms toward the Fairmaster. His hands open and close, as if reaching for his mother. "Cajole!" Fairmaster Beguile scolds. And just as quickly, the cries cease, and Artifice drives the boy out of his head.

"Very nice, son. Who's next?" Artifice says. Ruse steps forward. She angles her face down and tilts her eyes to muster a hard stare. Artifice boldly leaps atop the Fairmaster's desk with a smile reaching his ears. Everyone freezes. He gallantly spreads his arms out wide and begins to tap his feet in a jovial dance. Ruse claps, giggling, while the rest of the students share smiles and whispered comments. Before long, Artifice's hardened expression returns. He holds out his spindly hand to the Fairmaster who helps him down. A mild scowl crosses his face.

Soon, only Duplicity and I are left. "Next?" he says. Duplicity hasn't even reached the front by the time she has taken control of him. His eyes glaze over, and tears pool in the corners. His knuckles grip the desk with such force they are absent of color. "No! Please stop!" he cries out. He shakes his head violently and cowers into a crouched position.

"Duplicity! Enough!" Fairmaster Beguile shrieks. Duplicity's face softens and she snaps her fingers. Artifice sucks in a sharp breath followed by a couple of disturbed blinks. He rises to his feet and straightens his robes, glaring at Duplicity under a rigid brow. He looks away without a word.

"Jane?" he finally says. I stiffen. My legs manage to shuffle me to the front, and I stand before him. He looks down his long nose at me. I draw in a deep breath. Our eyes lock. "Go ahead, Jane," he says. *Okay. Think of something small...* I clear everything from my mind and concentrate on his formidable stare. Everyone waits. *Tug your ear. Tug your ear. Tug your ear.* I lean in closer and closer until I'm on my tiptoes, nearly nose-to-nose with him.

"That's quite enough," Fairmaster Beguile says, "Surely, your proximity is making him uncomfortable." I break my stare and exit his personal space. *How embarrassing. I'm ready to crawl into a corner and die now.*

Artifice makes a face. "Right. Good job today, my young tempters. You are the future of our Offering, so make me proud. Let's go ahead and take a recess. Duplicity and Jane, please stay behind."

The class races out while Duplicity drags her feet toward us. "Duplicity, since you are top of your class, we would like for you to tutor Jane," Fairmaster Beguile suggests.

"What? Absolutely not. Is this because of my tempting today? That's not fair—"

"It wasn't a question," Artifice cuts in sternly, "and it isn't a punishment. You should feel honored to help your fellow tempter in need." Duplicity scowls at me without a reply.

"Please, I don't need a tutor. I know my Offering will come in. The three foreseers have assured me. I promise I will practice extra hard. I can do this on my own," I plead.

Artifice and Fairmaster Beguile exchange skeptical glances. "We just want to keep an eye on you, Jane…and to help resolve any…issues," Artifice says. His long nose scrunches in disapproval.

Fairmaster Beguile sighs irritably. "Winter break. That's it. If your *abnormality* hasn't cleared up by then, Duplicity will tutor you until your Offering comes in."

"But–," Duplicity begins to protest.

"And that's final. You are dismissed," the Fairmaster says.

NINE

I HALF-LISTEN TO THE FAIRMASTER. I'm so far behind my class I've given up trying, and they waste no time moving on without me. No one wants to be my partner when we group up for activities and exercises. Even the Fairmaster doesn't know what to do with me. I just keep my head down and try to stay out of everyone's way.

"As I was saying," Fairmaster Beguile raises her voice, "You should all be planning how you will demonstrate your Offering for the Trials. Don't procrastinate. That's all for today. See you all bright and early tomorrow."

I get right to work on a load of dishes that have been piling up at home. I hum away a familiar tune Mother used to sing during mundane chores while I scrub. I strive to hit all the high notes but fall short more than a few times. Mother had been a much better singer.

Knock. Knock.

I choke on the tune and drop a wooden bowl into the basin. My head slowly turns toward the door. A paralyzing fear creeps up my spine as I imagine it enlarging into a monstrous size, daring to devour me. I haven't been bothered by the Elders for well over two months. *Why would they be starting their investigation back up again? And how can they accuse Mother of dishonesty when she isn't even here to defend herself?*

I have let it all go and moved on. But something as simple as a sturdy knock stirs all the awful feelings right back up. Mother's death...her deceit...mysterious notes, with little sympathy from anyone.

Or, maybe, they're here because of my school troubles. Another topic I'll pass on. I let out a deep breath. "You don't know anything, and you haven't done anything wrong," I affirm aloud. I crack the door. "I already told you that if I found—"

"Hey, Jane. What are you up to?" Remedy asks, leaning casually against the railing.

"Oh...it's just you." Relief washes over me as I open the door wider.

"Just me? Who were you expecting?"

"No one. I'm just glad it's you. Wait—how do you know where I live?"

"Are you kidding me? The infamous Sibyl's house? It's practically a landmark."

"Yeah, right," I say, blushing. "Seriously, how?"

"Okay—okay. I asked around at school. Your Fairmaster overheard me on the deck and offered me directions."

"Oh." *Is there anything that woman didn't see when she read my mind?*

"Is that okay?"

"Of course. I was just cleaning up. Please come in."

"Actually, I was kind of hoping you would come out with me."

"Sure. What did you have in mind?" I ask, grabbing my leather jacket off its wall hook.

"The Tavern?"

"Your parents let you go to the Tavern?"

"Well, no…not exactly. But they think I'm studying," Remedy says, pulling my arm to usher me outside.

After our trek, we hover at the entrance, looking for the best way to cross the room. It is an entirely different scene from my previous visit. The tables have been pushed out from the center to make space for dancing. Men play upbeat tunes on wooden flutes and lyres in the corner. My eyes float to Storm seated at the bar. I lead Remedy through the crowd to two open seats next to him. He looks dapper in fitted trousers and a dress shirt, but his wild mane of hair is flowing every which way.

"Hello, Jane and R-Remedy, is it?" he stutters, gawking.

She titters softly. "It is."

Her tone sounds flirtatious to me, but I'm no expert in romance. "Remedy, let me formally introduce you to my new friend, Storm."

"Nice to meet you, Storm," she says, eyes twinkling. Her cheeks blush as she smooths her hand over her heart and kindly holds it out to him. His movements are quick as he mimics her actions and gently slides his hand against hers.

"I saw what you did for Duplicity at the cliffs. That was nice of you," he says. He holds her gaze for a few moments before realizing her hand is still prisoner to his grip. He releases her hand suddenly and clears his throat. "What brings you two out here on a school night?"

"School has been keeping us busy, but we could use a break," Remedy says, nudging me with a playful smile.

"So, what's going on in here? And why are you all dressed up?" I ask him.

"It happens to be Blossom's birthday," he says, scooping a large mug off the bar and raising it in her direction. "And she's not a day over seventy!"

"Happy birthday!" I shout over the music. Blossom smirks and continues pouring mugs. I grab a couple of pints off the counter and hand one to Remedy. "Now, be careful, these things can be dangerous. Trust me."

Duplicity swans inside, looking flashy in a blue dress with a plunging neckline. *Of course she'd be here.* The dress fits her form in all the right places. Augur is attached to her hip, wearing a matching blue open-collared shirt. Duplicity stomps over to a full table in the corner and glares at the seated guests. Her hands hike up to her hips. She clears her throat, and the browbeaten regulars quickly abandon their seats.

Duplicity and Augur begin canoodling as soon as their bottoms graze the chairs, subjecting everyone to their nauseating display of necking. Storm looks away and holds out his hand to Remedy. "Would you care to dance?"

"Do you mind?" Remedy asks me.

"Of course not. You two go ahead."

Remedy follows Storm to the dance floor hand in hand. He doesn't take his eyes off her, as they float around the floor intertwined. She has a warmth about her that comes from within, a quality missing in his old flame, Duplicity.

I watch them, seeing the sparks fly. I have never met a man that struck me in that way. Who knows if I ever will? But I know I want to experience whatever it is I see in Remedy's eyes as Storm dips her and brings her back upright. He twirls her and pulls her in close, resting her hand against his robust chest.

"Aren't you going to ask me to dance?" Duplicity shrieks at Augur, loud enough for everyone to hear. A hard elbow to his side makes him choke on his drink.

"Of course, my love," he squeaks between coughs.

Duplicity shoots to her feet and drags him over near Remedy and Storm. "Twirl me!" She jerks Augur's hand in the air and flings herself into a twirl, whipping her mane of red locks across Remedy's face. She tosses Augur around the dance floor in aggressive strides. His face pains as he tries his best to keep up.

As they round a full revolution of the dance floor, Duplicity collides a hard shoulder with Remedy without even breaking stride. Remedy clutches her arm. "Excuse you!" she shouts after them, but they have already fluttered back across the room.

"Really, Augur? Do you have to do that now? I look fantastic. Twirl me," Duplicity shouts above the music. Augur is unresponsive, feet fused in place. His eyes gloss over—I know that look. Mother wore that face daily. After three hazy blinks, he breaks free from Duplicity's grasp and marches over to Storm, tapping him hard on the shoulder.

Storm turns toward a red-faced Augur. "What's up, man? Is there a problem?"

"Meet me outside," Augur barks and flounces out the door. Storm's forehead scrunches, but he follows him with me, Remedy, and Duplicity at his heels.

"I just saw you kissing my girlfriend, Storm! You lowlife snake!" Augur shouts.

"I don't know what you're talking about. And you might want to get some practice under your belt before you go around trying to pick fights. You don't know who you're messing with," Storm says.

"That's impossible. I would never go back to Storm," Duplicity snaps.

Augur throws his hand up, all but telling her to keep her mouth shut. "It hasn't happened yet, but it's going to! I saw it! You can't tell me you don't still have feelings for Duplicity! I've seen the way you look at her!" Augur screams.

"Are you serious? You're going to yell at me for something that hasn't even happened yet? You can't even be sure that it will. Trust me, I'm not interested." I grab Storm's arm and try to pull him back inside but it's useless. He does not budge. "Everything is fine, Jane. Go wait for me with Remedy," Storm orders, eyes locked on Augur.

I fold my arms and reluctantly step back next to Remedy. Duplicity's lips curve up just enough to prove she is thrilled to watch two men so emotionally charged over her. "Is this barfly who you want to be with?" Augur asks her.

"No. I love you, Augur. He's a pathetic weatherman."

"There, you heard her! She doesn't want you. Now back off. If you know what's good for you," Augur threatens.

Storm laughs in disbelief. "You better run along, little schoolboy, before I teach you a lesson." His muscular build dwarfs Augur's lean body as he steps closer, accepting the challenge. Augur shakes with rage. His fists tighten and the veins of his arms bulge. Storm just smirks, looking exceptionally relaxed.

Augur lunges forward but stops short for intimidation. Storm doesn't flinch, but his smirk fades into a hard line. "Just because you're puny doesn't mean I'm going to go easy on you. This is your last chance to walk away."

Augur holds his ground. Storm raises one shoulder and lowers it. "I guess we're doing this." He points his index finger down and blazes a stream of fire to encircle them. They both shift around the ring, guarded, waiting for an opening to strike.

"Come on!" Augur shouts. Storm grits his teeth and plows forward, unleashing a furious right jab. Augur ducks hard left. The angry fist whooshes by, just missing his cheek. Augur stands up straight with big eyes. A pleased grin stretches across his face. Storm tries to fake him out by springing right and rebounding with a sudden left hook. Augur weaves away with nimble ease. Storm bulldozes forward swinging wildly, but Augur effortlessly evades his combos.

"AHH!" Storm shouts toward the sky. A thunderous crack splits the horizon, and rain pelts down from above. The circle of fire billows into smoke.

"You think that's going to help you?" Augur yells, shaking the rain from his curls. Storm squats to the ground and sweeps his leg under, but Augur is already airborne in a barrel turn. He lands back on his feet lightly. "You've already lost," he adds.

Storm charges him once more but slips on the wet ground. He tumbles forward. "There it is," Augur says, cocking back to hurl his right fist. He leans into the punch with all his might. His knuckles connect with Storm's chin mid-fall, slamming him to the ground on his back. The rain stops.

Augur steps over Storm's limp body with his head held high. "Foreseer…remember?" he says, and spits just shy of Storm's vacant stare. He interlocks his arm in Duplicity's with renewed confidence, and they march triumphantly into the forest without so much as another look back.

Remedy kneels beside Storm and cradles his head, mopping up the blood with her hands. She traces her dainty fingers over his temples as her healing power pulses throughout his skull. He cracks his eyes and groans in defeat. "Are you okay?" I ask. "He got you pretty good."

"Yeah, thanks to Remedy, here," he says, smiling up at her. "Although, my pride is hardly intact."

"Not much I can do about that, unfortunately," she chuckles. We help him to his feet and brush the dirt off him.

"I have no interest in Duplicity. He was way off," Storm assures us. "I better go get cleaned up. It was a pleasure to meet you, Remedy. You girls enjoy the rest of your evening." His head is low as he breaks away from us to head home.

"He's cute, huh? Even if he did lose the fight," Remedy admits once he's gone.

"I knew it! You have a crush on Storm."

"I wouldn't mind getting to know him better is all," she says with a wink. Coming to a fork in the moonlit trail, we exchange hugs and say our goodbyes. I don't notice it at first, but by the time I plop into bed my cheeks are aching. For the first time since Mother passed, I have reason to smile—friends.

TEN

AS THE FOREST GROWS DREARY beneath the gray skies of
winter, I can hardly wait for the Winter Solstice. The Fairkind celebrate the occurrence annually, gathering for a grand feast
to commemorate the shortest day of the year. (It should be noted
that we tend to skip over the summer solstice. Our people cannot
find cause to celebrate the longest day. And who can blame us?
We live hundreds of years.) Not to mention, the time off from
school that comes with it—a break I desperately need. I am trying
my best to ignore the impending doom that awaits me afterward,
though. *Tutoring. Duplicity.*

When the day of the feast finally arrives, I dress in a golden
gown of silk and Mother's finest boots for the occasion, wrapping
myself tightly in a fox fur. It has been freezing all week with no
signs of warming anytime soon. I head out the door, toting a small
pie from one of Mother's old recipes. The scent of hot cranberries
and mulled spices trails behind me until I reach the glade.

The moon is already overhead, and dozens of torches glow
through flurries of snow. Long wooden tables are marked with

large candelabras at each end. Soft tealights twinkle around the heaping platters of food. A cheerful hum rings in the air.

Mouthwatering treats and cuisines parade before my eyes in every direction. The ducks are golden-brown. Thick slabs of succulent boar glisten in a moist honey glaze, garnished with pineapple rounds. The savory venison soaks in its juices, becoming more tender by the minute. Fruit and vegetable trays are sprawled out next to loaves of bread with spreads and cheeses.

My stomach growls loudly. I glance around to make sure no one is watching before wiping some dribble escaping the corners of my mouth. *Phew. That could've been embarrassing.*

I come to the assortment of desserts, standing beside a conditioner applying finishing touches to her dish. She sprinkles some sugar over a platter of mini custards and blasts them afire with her fingertip. The sugar melts into a layer of golden bubbles. I wait for the woman to walk away before adding my humble pie to the selection. That's when I spot Storm and Remedy nearby and sneak up behind them. "What's going on over here?!"

"Jane! You scared me. And don't you look pretty," Remedy says, turning around to give me a big squeeze.

"Well, no one is going to notice me—standing next to you," I say, looking her up and down. Remedy's long-sleeved red velvet dress is hard to ignore against the pale snow.

"I'm already on my third cup of spiked cider. You two better catch up," Storm says as I take a seat across from him. He looks handsome as always, but remarkably tidier.

"I think we know who the real lush is," I tease him.

"To be fair, most of the time when you see me, I'm winding down from a hard day's work," he says defensively.

"You better slow down. Jane and I aren't strong enough to carry you home," Remedy says.

"Shh. Gust is about to give his toast," Storm says, nodding toward the Elder as he makes his way to the front. The other

Elders' silhouettes are lost in their cloaks, but Gust is so brawny that even his navy garb can't hide his big muscles. I have always considered him to be good-looking but standing next to Artifice and Herald, there's hardly competition.

"Greetings, my fellow Fairkind." His deep, burly voice quiets everyone. "We've had an excellent harvest this year. Join me in partaking of this feast and remember to be thankful and kind to one another, on this night and always. Cheers! Enjoy the feast!" Gust lifts his oversized mug to the sky. He takes a big swig, and the crowd does the same.

"Who did the ice sculpture this year?" Remedy asks after wolfing down most of her plate.

"Ash volunteered, but he's a procrastinator. I doubt it will be as good as mine was last year," Storm replies in between bites of potatoes and cabbage. He leans in and lowers his voice. "Want to go have a sneak peek?"

"Are you sure that's a good idea?" I ask.

"Yeah, it'll be our little secret." His pointer finger slides over his lips. Storm leads the way, zipping between tables to the front. We stand there faking small talk and looking around for watching eyes for a couple of minutes. "Okay, now." He grabs our wrists and pulls us behind the curtain that hides the sculpture from the audience.

It is massive. The faces of the five Elders have been carved into the block of ice with precision. Every wrinkle, crease, and dimple are all accounted for. The heads are stacked one on top of the other with Artifice on top, of course. "It's...incredible," I say.

"Yeah, Storm, this is pretty good," Remedy agrees.

"Not too bad for the little weasel, I have to say," he says with a tone of genuine surprise. "Alright, we got the first look. You girls ready for some dessert?"

"Why don't we walk around a bit?" Remedy suggests. I can see a slight twinkle in her eye.

"Okay, but let's sneak out the back so nobody catches us," he says. We creep out and make our way under a large redwood off in the outer reaches. We stand there for a few peaceful moments in silence, watching the spirited party.

I catch Storm breaking his gaze now and then to sneak glimpses of Remedy. "On second thought, I saw some custards earlier that are calling my name. I'll catch up with you two back at the table," I say, making eyes at Storm while discreetly jerking my head toward Remedy. When I am a little way off from them, I turn back to eavesdrop.

My timing could not have been more perfect. Storm shifts his weight onto his left foot to lean in closer to Remedy and slips on a slick sheet of icy ground. He clumsily tries to regain his balance, then falls flat on his face. I have to hold my breath to keep from laughing.

"Are you okay? That was a nasty fall," Remedy says, bending down to help him to his feet.

"Yeah. Watch your step, though." He wipes the snow from his mouth with his thumb. "Ouch." A gash splits his bottom lip. Blood immediately drips from his face.

"You're hurt," Remedy says. "Here, be still." She closes her eyes and leans in to place a delicate kiss on his lips. She lingers against him and pulls away slowly.

His face lights up. Whether it is from the kiss or his restored lip I can't say. "I think I'll keep you around," he says.

I smile to myself and quietly continue back to the party. After I finish off a plate of sweets, Storm and Remedy return with interlocked hands and big smiles. "Well, aren't you two cute," I say as they reclaim their seats across from me.

"Hardly," Duplicity snarks, coming up behind them. Her black dress clings to her body so snugly that I can make out each of her ribs. It is low-cut with slits up to her thighs. The sleeves are long but made of a very thin black lace.

"Aren't you a little underdressed? It's freezing," I scoff.

"You wish you could pull this off. But there would be nothing to hold up the front, *Plainssss Jane*," Duplicity snaps, scrutinizing my modest chest. My cheeks burn as I clench down on my bottom teeth. "Storm, we need to talk," she says, tugging on his forearm.

He yanks his arm away. "I don't think so."

"It will only take a minute. Please," she persists.

Storm eyes Remedy, but she nods for him to go ahead. He sighs. "Fine." And follows Duplicity off to the side.

"I need a refill after that. Would you like one?" I ask Remedy, rising to stand.

"Does Duplicity look like a floozy?"

I burst into unrestrained laughter. "Two refills it is."

I inspect the various drink selections at the beverage table, even sniffing a bizarre, fizzy one I'm curious about. "…Here I am. Get on with it then," Storm barks within earshot. I peek over at him from the corner of my eye.

"I'll admit it. I'm a little jealous," Duplicity says.

"Is that what this is about?"

"You got my attention, Storm," she says, puckering her lips.

"I'm not trying to get your attention, Duplicity. I'm interested in someone else."

"Let me remind you how interesting I am." My eyebrows shoot into my forehead as she grabs his face and presses her plump lips into his.

Storm clutches Duplicity's shoulders and backs away from her. "What about your new boyfriend? Where is Augur, by the way?"

"Don't worry about him," she says, taking another step toward him.

"That must have been the kiss he saw." *Wait. That means Augur is powerful enough to see other people's futures. And he hasn't even finished school yet.*

Duplicity shrugs. "Who cares?" She stands on her tippy-toes and leans into him again.

"No. I've moved on. You should too." He turns his back to her and marches toward our table.

I snatch a couple of hot chocolates and rush back to my seat, Storm nearly beating me back. "So, what was that all about?" Remedy asks him.

"Don't worry. I took care of it. But basically..."

An old, boisterous grower named Bud comes up to me while Storm brings Remedy up to speed on the developing Duplicity drama. Bud is completely bald with a permanently hunched back from his constant poor posture. A gray beard covers his lower face, which he makes a point to keep neatly trimmed. He's nearing three centuries but still has the smile of a child as he grins at me.

"Good evening, young Jane," he says, using a wooden cane to ease himself into an empty seat. "I've been meaning to come see you for some time now, but you know me. An old man, such as I, hardly finds the time to leave his own tree."

I smile back at him. "That's okay, Bud." He adjusts in his seat with a small yelp and groans. "Why haven't you been to see a healer? You're in pain," I say.

"Young lady, mark my words. There will come a time when you feel just as I do. I've been around for a long time. Seen many things, and I'm ready to move beyond this life." His words have me pondering if there is another form of existence that follows death. *I hope so.* No one knows where the orbs of our souls are taken, except for those who have already gone on ahead of us.

"You sound like my mother," I say. My eyes well up and I change the subject. "So, how've you been? I've missed you."

"Well enough." His face droops. "I catch myself thinking about Sibyl often."

The edges of my lips turn down slightly at the mention of her name—a new reflex I'm noticing. "What comes to mind when you think of her?"

"Good golly, plenty of things. But she only ever mused over two matters, you know. Her big plans—plans I've never quite understood, mind you—and you, Jane. I've never seen another soul love anyone or thing in that manner." He pats me softly on the head.

Tears trickle down the sides of my face. "I miss her, too." Storm pulls a handkerchief from his pocket and hands it to me. "Thanks," I say, dabbing my eyes. "What sort of plans would she talk about?"

"Who can say? Sibyl wasn't exactly forthcoming." *There go my lips again.* "But she was convinced that something had been set in motion. Something she was somehow wrapped up in." He sighs. "I'm sorry. I wish I knew more."

It takes me a moment to realize that Remedy is no longer seated with us. I glance around but don't see any sign of her. I end up spotting Fairmaster Beguile seated closer to the front. She looks uncomfortable in her plum-colored dress, undoubtedly the only thing of color in her entire wardrobe. We meet eyes briefly and she forces a smile, tugging on her frilly sleeves that keep falling off her shoulders.

Gust marches back to the front and stands next to the curtains draping the sculpture. "As you've all been anticipating, the time has come to reveal this year's ice sculpture, carved by our very own Ash. But, before we get to that, I'm told we have a special announcement."

Augur staggers up to the front with a giddiness about him. His hair has been tamed into tight ringlets, not nearly as frizzy as normal. He loosens his dress scarf and puffs out his chest. "Good evening, friends and family. I…um…wanted to take this opportunity to share what I hope will be the best day of my life, with you all. Duplicity, would you come up here, please?"

Duplicity smiles uneasily as she joins Augur at the front. He grasps her hands and says, "These past few months have made me happier than I ever thought I could be. Every day you challenge me to be greater than I was the day before. Please make me the happiest man in the world by saying yes…" He pulls a spectacular diamond ring from his pocket. The stone's luster shimmers to the very rear of the crowd. "Will you marry me?"

Duplicity's jaw drops open. "Oh, Augur!" She lunges at him, wrapping her arms tightly around his neck.

"So, will you have me?" he manages to say before she secures him in a chokehold.

"Yes! Yes! Of course, yes! I love you so much!" Duplicity releases him, and Augur slides the ring on her finger. A chorus of applause fills the party.

"Ahh! Look at the size of that thing!" Ruse shouts as she springs toward the newly betrothed couple. She cradles Duplicity's left hand in her grasp to eyeball the jewel, practically drooling.

"Maybe now she'll stop harassing us," Storm whispers.

"Let's hope. Have you seen Remedy?"

"She wanted to say hello to a friend from her class but that was a while ago. We should probably go look for her," he says.

"And now, without further ado, the unveiling!" Gust bellows. The curtain is pulled back on his cue and my heart falls through my stomach. Horrified gasps and screams from the crowd ensue in waves. The sculpture has been transformed into something different. The only face displayed now is that of my friend, Remedy, her expression frozen in terror as she remains trapped inside the block of ice.

I bulldoze through the crowd right up to Duplicity and shove her to the ground. "How could you?!"

Fairmaster Beguile is quick to jump in between us. "We need to focus on your friend right now," she tells me. Gust melts the ice and gently lays Remedy on the ground while Storm radiates heat into her frosted body. Curative massages her fingers along Remedy's skin to try and revive her.

Remedy's parents come forward to crouch around their daughter, both a mess of tears. We are out of time, and nothing seems to be helping. I start to see the all-too-familiar glow in her chest. "Please, Remedy, don't go," I cry.

"Stand back!" Storm shouts. "I hope this works. *Please work.*" His hand trembles as he places it over Remedy's chest and releases a jolt of electricity. Her body jerks under the current, but before long the light of death dulls until it vanishes entirely.

Remedy's blue lips quiver. "She's back!" he shouts. He exhales hard and pulls her in close, warming her as she rests in his arms. The color returns to her cheeks and her eyes split open. Storm steadies her while she finds her footing to stand. He seizes her, cradling her in a tight embrace. Her eyes brim with tears as he gently rocks her back and forth. When their bodies part, Storm wags a finger in front of her eyes to dry them without even touching her. "Don't worry, I'll keep you safe," he whispers. "Who did this to you?"

"D-Duplicity and Ash," Remedy stammers.

"I'm so sorry, Remedy. Please forgive me," Ash says, hanging his head. He points to Duplicity. "She must have tempted me!"

Duplicity shrinks into the crowd to cower behind Augur. "Duplicity! Come forward!" Gust roars, his broad shoulders shaking with fury. Augur escorts her to where the Elders stand, unable to contain his baffled expression.

"What have you to say for yourself?" Curative asks her.

"It was only supposed to be a prank. I didn't know Augur was going to propose and delay the unveiling."

"She almost died!" Storm shouts, his clenched fists shaking at his sides.

Gust places a comforting hand on Storm's shoulder. "Let us handle this." Remedy's parents stand by silently, guarding their daughter with unforgiving stances.

"I'm afraid this girl has a troubled future," Omen calls, edging closer from the fringes of the throng. *Um, you think?!* Artifice is noticeably cross by the remark.

"Tell us what you see in store for her, Herald," Gust urges. Duplicity's parents snake closer.

"It's not entirely clear. It's shrouded in darkness," Herald replies with shifty eyes, trying to gauge Artifice's expression.

"We cannot tolerate this kind of behavior. She must suffer the repercussions of her actions, and they should be equally severe," Curative says. Artifice says nothing, but his face objects. The Elders turn amongst themselves to discuss the matter in private. The crowd pulses with anxious murmurs.

"We have reached a judgment. Majority rules that Duplicity shall be detained in our custody for her misconducts against her fellow Fairkind," Gust declares.

"She's a good girl! She meant no harm! Please, don't take away our only child," Duplicity's mother begs.

"Yes, please reconsider. Duplicity is one of the most talented tempters I have ever had the pleasure to teach. She has great potential," Fairmaster Beguile adds. *You would say that.*

"That may be true, but we cannot be certain that potential won't be used for corruption. We will not dismiss this transgression," Ginger says, folding her arms over her chest.

"Let her stay!" Ruse yells across the crowd.

"After what she's done? No way!" I argue.

Artifice holds up his hand, and everyone falls silent. "Duplicity shall remain in my charge. Consequently, she will not be permitted to compete in the Tourney this spring," he says matter-of-factly.

Ginger huffs, visibly irritated by Artifice's leniency. "We must also ask that you depart from the celebration, out of respect for Remedy. Furthermore, I believe an apology is in order," she says.

Duplicity clicks her tongue with a blank face. She says nothing until, at last, Augur squeezes her hand tightly. "Sorry," she mumbles.

ELEVEN

O N THE DAY WE ARE to return to school, I arrive very early
to the Redwoods. It's strange to see the deck empty, without the bustle of chattering students. "Good morning, Fairmaster.
Sorry to disturb you so early," I say, poking my head in the doorway.

Fairmaster Beguile looks up from the stacks of parchment
on her desk. "Jane, what a surprise. What can I do for you?"

"I'm honestly still a bit shaken up by what happened to Remedy. And—not to tattle—but that wasn't the first time Duplicity
has bullied us. Would you mind if I took an extra day from class
to clear my head?"

Fairmaster Beguile sets her quill down and purses her lips into a hard line. "You may take the day, but you will be sharing a
class with her for the duration of your training. I suggest you make
peace with that. You of all people need to be in school to practice." I look down at my feet, ashamed.

"I've been going easy on you, but you are failing my class.
And remember, you'll be pairing up with Duplicity for tutoring.
You can learn a lot from her and the two of you should use this

opportunity to work out your differences. Come back tomorrow ready to work," she says.

"Okay. Thank you." I hurry down the stairs and disappear into the dense forest. I push through a fair distance of rough terrain until Storm's young redwood is in view. The door swings open, and he steps out onto his balcony.

"Aren't you supposed to be in school?" he calls down to me.

"I'm playing hooky today. Want to hang out?"

Storm slouches over the railing. "Can't. I've got patrol duty."

"Mind if I tag along?"

"I guess, but it's going to be boring." He holds his hands out in front of him and concentrates. A forceful wind swirls between his palms until he parts his hands wide, and a cloud develops. He plops on top and floats down to me.

"No offense, but I'd prefer to walk," I say.

"No can do. I'm patrolling the boundary today. It would take days to get there on foot." Storm smirks and pats the seat behind him.

My jaw clenches. I force a smile and slowly ease onto the cloud. "Hold on!" he says. I latch onto him tight. He snaps his fingers and cues a blast of wind that thrusts us up to the treeline.

The taste of the thick, salty air strikes me as we propel swiftly through the sky. I peer down, watching our shadows glide over the coast. Conditioners wade in the water beneath us, casting their crude nets. They lead the fish into the shallows by controlling the currents with their hands.

One of them stands on the shore fileting each catch. Gulls circle over his head, screeching for a handout. The man pays them no mind as he grabs an empty wicker basket and scoops it full of seawater. With a quick shake, the water freezes into chunks of ice. He lays the filets on top.

"Look out there," Storm says, pointing further offshore. Many other conditioners paddle furiously toward the shore. A large wave crests over them and they spring from the water, surfing the wave on their bare feet.

"Brrr! Must be nice to be a conditioner and warm yourself when it's so chilly!" I shout through chattering teeth. *I'll be surprised if he understood that.*

"Oh, sorry. Didn't think about that." His body instantly heats to warm me as I hug his back. When we finally reach the outskirts of our realm, the cloud lowers and dissipates, gently setting our feet on the ground. There is a large shoulder-high thicket of thorns to signify the boundary line. It stretches all the way around our side of the forest.

"I've never been this far out before. Have you ever seen a human out here?" I ask.

"Nope."

"But others have seen them?"

Storm rolls his eyes. "So they say…but there hasn't been a sighting in a while."

"I see their big, stiff birds with tails of smoke all the time."

"Yeah, me too. Luckily, the forest canopy offers us enough covering from the sky. So…have you heard anything about Remedy? I've been worried about her."

"I was wondering how long you'd last without bringing her up…longer than I expected, honestly," I say with a grin. "But yeah, she's fine, just rattled is all." I pause and squint into the woods across the boundary. "I think I hear voices," I whisper.

Storm strains to listen. "Good ear. It's probably someone else on patrol. They always have about twenty or so of us out here making the rounds. Kind of pointless if you ask me. I think we've had a few bear sightings. Bobcats here and there, but those things are terrified of us."

"Shh!" I yank him to the ground. "It's the humans!" They are about a quarter of a mile away but easily spotted sporting the most visually assaulting orange vests. Oddly enough, the clothing they wear underneath blends in with the forest exactly.

"Are you sure they're human?" he asks.

"Well, seeing how they're on the other side of our border, I'd say so!"

"What do we do? They're headed straight for us!" Storm blabbers.

"You're asking me?! Haven't you trained for this? We're dead! Can't you just fog them out or something—so they can't see us? Do something, Storm!" He crawls behind a large tree and lifts his arms, rolling out thick vapors from his fingertips.

The humans stumble at the sudden onset of fog, nearly suffocated by the vapor. They all turn back except for one, who trudges forward in the direction of the thicket. Another patrolman sprints into a hard slide over to Storm. "Hey, man, is everything okay?" he asks in a low voice.

Drenched in sweat, Storm musters up a shaky whisper. "Three humans—one is still headed this way. I need your help, Con."

"No kidding? A human?! I've always wanted to see one. Just move over to the left some and stay low. I'm going to have to make contact. But keep the fog coming!" Storm ducks back down to hide next to me but continues to pump out thick blankets. I crouch in place and hold my knees to keep them from shaking.

Con is calm as he approaches the thicket and shouts over the wall, "Hey!" The man jerks his head toward him, startled. "You're a long way from home. Aren't you, human?"

The man raises a narrow, black contraption toward the sky. "We don't want any trouble, but we got guns, ya hear?" he exclaims. A reverberating bang cuts through the forest.

*"**Turn around and go home. You will forget this place and never return,**"* Con says to the man. The stranger's eyes widen and

lock onto Con's. With a slow exaggerated nod, the human turns around in a trance-like motion and walks away.

Storm and I crawl out of hiding. "Thanks for having my back, man," Storm says, wiping the sweat from his brow.

"Anytime!" Con chirps.

"What in the world was that thing he was carrying—that made that loud bang?" I ask.

"Some kind of weapon. He wasn't planning on using it unless we attacked him. Still, I better alert the others about what we saw. Keep your guard up and holler if you need me." He turns back in the direction he came.

"I can't believe that just happened. Humans! Can you believe it? It was kind of cool, though, right? They sounded so much scarier in folktales," I ramble on excitedly.

"Well, I was scared! Gust told me if they ever discovered us, they'd torture us."

"What makes him say that?"

"One time, he saw some of them huddled around a freshly slain deer carcass. A doe. One of their young tore the still-beating heart from its chest and ravaged it like an animal. Ripping chunk after chunk with his teeth."

"Ew. That's disgusting."

"That's not even the worst part. Get this, then he smears the warm blood all over his face. I mean, how sick is that? And all the while, the adults are cheering him on and clapping him on the back for his savagery."

"That's horrible."

"Yeah—no kidding. Just imagine what those barbarians would do to us."

"I guess you're right. But, wow, I had no idea how much they looked like us. Why do you think that is? They don't have Offerings, right?"

Storm raises one shoulder and lowers it. "All I know is, we don't mess with them, and they don't know about us."

"Do you ever wonder what's beyond our land? Like, what else is out there?" I point far past the thicket.

"No. Some stones are better left unturned. Speaking of which, I have something for you," he says, reaching into his pocket. "The larger sapphire is for you, and the smaller one is for Remedy. You see her more than I do. I figured these could help you two with the Tourney, and you're allowed to use them. Yours is a blast of wind, strong enough to knock a few big guys off their feet. Remedy's is a strike of lightning...you know, to remind her of how I saved her life." He winks and places the gems in my hand.

"Thanks, Storm. I'm glad we're friends." He claps me lightly on the shoulder and yanks me under his armpit for a hug. "So, how do I win this thing? Any tricks? I need to show Fairmaster Beguile that I'm not as incompetent as everyone thinks."

"Every year is completely unpredictable. But you don't want to come off too strong in the beginning—that was my mistake. Pace yourself."

TWELVE

I TILT MY HEAD BACK to get a good look at Duplicity's home. It has multiple wings, spanning across three giant redwoods. A large terrace links the three trunks, with a staircase coming off each tree.

I climb the stairs in the center and eye the large double wooden doors at the top. A frown pulls at my lips as I gently graze a pair of antler tines jutting from the door as handles. Muted chatter drifts from inside, so I quietly lean my ear against the door.

"I still see your potential for greatness and would like to prime you as my successor, but your temper tends to get the better of you. As an Elder, it is important to maintain a spotless image. Do you understand what I'm telling you?" the garbled voice of Artifice echoes through the door.

"Yes, but now that Augur has asked me to marry him, how is that still possible for me?" Duplicity asks him.

"Everything is still very unofficial at this point, so we must keep things hush-hush. But I've been in communication with the other Elders, and I think it's time we put that ludicrous law to rest. They don't all agree, just yet, but I'm certain they will concede to me. I'm getting older and will soon be ready to retire my seat. But I need your full cooperation. It's imperative that I can trust you."

"You can trust me, Artifice."

"Excellent. I must admit, I've always been rather partial to you, Duplicity. You're like the daughter I never had." *Strange thing for an Elder to say.* "Now, I've already spoken with Fairmaster Beguile, and I understand you'll be tutoring Jane. What can you tell me about her?"

"She's hopeless. I've never seen someone so weak. I have no idea how she was ever placed as a tempter. She's not like us at all."

"Do you really believe that she hasn't come into her Offering yet?"

"She hasn't. I know that for a fact." Having heard enough, I make a tight fist and knock hard on the door. Their voices silence, replaced by shuffling sounds. Someone stomps toward the door. Duplicity swings it open, draped in attitude with her hand on her hip. "You made it. Might as well come in and get started. We have our work cut out for us."

I smile curtly and step inside, gawping at the flashy decorating. A moose head is mounted to the wall above the hearth, and three large rubies—each the size of my head—rest in the center of a polished mahogany table. A huge bearskin rug is spread across the floor—head still intact. Large fangs hang from the bear's gaping jaw. I cover my mouth, stomach churning from the grisly sight. *Her family is worse than the humans.*

Duplicity notices my gaze and brags, "Took him down last week. I tempted him to lay still so I could open him up with my knife. My parents have never been so proud." She beams and I give a slow nod, trying not to look directly at it.

"Hello, Jane," Artifice says. "I would like to monitor the tutoring session for a bit."

"That's fine. Shall we go outside and get started?" I ask, eager to get away from the animal carcasses.

"The terrace will be fine. Birds will be easier to spot from this height," Duplicity answers. She steps outside and commands a robin to fly down to the railing within seconds. Artifice stands by idly like a dark statue. "Okay, Jane, I'm about to release him. When I say so, you need to lock eyes with the bird until you feel connected to him—like an invisible tunnel linking your brain to his. Then you'll sense the expanded consciousness and impress your will over him," Duplicity states. I stare the bird down so intensely that I wonder if I'll burn a hole clear through him. "Okay, he's all yours!" The bird immediately shoots up into the tree canopy. "What was that?" Duplicity snaps.

"I'm trying, but I don't feel anything. I didn't even blink."

Duplicity shakes her head. "Let's find something slower to practice on," she grumbles, descending the stairs. "I'm going to make this as easy for you as possible." She bends down and overturns a large rock half-concealed under heavy moss.

Worms and beetles scatter, but Duplicity sets her eyes on a translucent salamander clinging to the bottom of the rock. "This ugly thing has big eyes for you to lock onto. And I want you to physically touch it, so you have another mode of connection." The creature wiggles between her fingers. My stomach flip-flops.

I gently pluck the salamander from her hand with my thumb and pointer finger. He twitches as I squeeze his slimy body. *Disgusting.* "What should I tempt it to do?"

"Make it crawl in a circle in the palm of your hand but form the connection before you let it go."

I hold the squirming salamander up at eye level. I glare at his glossy, black eyes intently until his body suddenly droops. I release my grip and flatten my palm. The salamander lies motionless, and I envision him creeping around my hand in my mind's eye. Duplicity and Artifice inch closer. "Oh wow! I think this might be it!" I squeal.

The salamander's tiny, sticky legs jiggle. The creature springs to his feet and catapults himself through the air, landing square on Artifice's whopping nose. "AHH!" A terrified cry rips from his thin lips, as he smacks himself in the face. Duplicity stifles a laugh. "You should never cause an animal to attack anyone!" Artifice shouts as he flings the salamander off him.

"I didn't do that! He jumped out of my hand. I promise!"

Artifice narrows his eyes. I feel his heavy presence enter my mind, verifying my story. *See? I told you so.* His nose twitches. "Right. Well, you have a long way to go before you'll be ready for the Trials."

"I know," I say sheepishly.

Artifice leaves and Duplicity shakes her head. "Seriously, what is wrong with you?"

I look away to hide the shame in my eyes. "I wish I knew."

THIRTEEN

T HE SUN RISES AND FALLS many times until the snow melts into young, green leaves. Spring has sprung, and the nip of winter is a faint memory. On the morning of the Tourney, I fly out of bed just before the sun hits the sky. I shovel down a hearty breakfast of warm oats and cane sugar and bolt down the stairs. The forest is dark and silent.

I know I don't stand a chance competing against my peers in the upcoming game because they have already learned how to wield their Offerings. *Maybe they won't notice me, they hardly ever do.* Then I remember the humans and an idea forms. Their camou-flaged clothes blended with the forest so well—apart from the orange vests, that is.

I comb around the foot of my tree, collecting small piles of leaves and twigs. Back upstairs, I scatter the brush over a dingy, brown shirt and trousers then stitch the plants into place. Going unseen can work to my advantage for once. After changing into my disguise, I duck behind the nearest tree, practicing my stealthy movements. I jog to the grounds of the playing field, erratically diving into bushes every so often.

A massive archway of large gemstones hangs gleaming above me as I enter the Tourney grounds. A high wall of thorns circles the playing field. The forest inside the wall is dark, even though the sun is now blazing down. Thick underbrush suffocates the trees, making it hard to see into the thick of it. There are five equidistant bases inside the edges of the thorn wall.

Wooden bleachers encircle the field, forming an audience for friends and family. They are already packed with spectators craning their necks to get a good look at the swarm of students. Remedy is on the ground stretching when our gaze meets. She jumps up and squeezes me tightly. "It's finally here. I'm so excited!"

"And Duplicity has to sit out for the whole thing," I remind her.

"I still can't believe she kissed Storm the night of the Solstice," she says, raising a sharp eyebrow.

"And the fact that she nearly murdered you?"

"Yeah, that either," Remedy chuckles.

"There's no line she won't cross. Especially when she's jealous."

Remedy nods. "So…can we talk about what you're wearing?" She looks over my leafy clothes with skepticism.

"Oh, right. Don't judge—I'm trying to be extra sneaky."

She smiles. "I think it's a great idea."

"You remembered to bring that lightning stone, right?"

"Yep. Got it right here." She pats her pants pocket. I pat mine too, just to be sure I didn't lose the one Storm gave me.

Fairmaster Beguile rounds up my class to make a few announcements. "Good morning, boys and girls. The purpose of the Tourney is to show how reliant we are on one another. Use your different strengths to combat your opponents. There are five bases in these woods, spread out over several acres. Each of the five teams is tasked with guarding a gemstone at their base. The first team to capture another team's stone, without having lost their own, wins. Elder Ginger has erected a wall of thorns around the grounds. Crossing over this wall automatically disqualifies you and will leave your team a player short. Make no mistake, this will be dangerous. You may very well be injured in some way. That's why healers are also very important in the game. You may use your Offerings, as well as any gemstones you have acquired, to deflect other teams' advances, but deadly force is strictly prohibited. The names of the winning team will be etched into the captured stone, to be displayed forevermore. So, keep an eye out for the stones of winners from years past," she says.

"Now, since we won't be having class today, here's a list of essential skills that you all should be excelling at by now. Read over it and take inventory of what needs your attention." The Fairmaster passes out copies of the list to the students. I skim it over:

Two Kinds of Tempting:

1. Figments
2. Commands

Different Mediums to Tempt:

1. Animals
2. Fairkind

    • Tempting a non-tempter
    • Tempting a tempter

3. Humans (Rarely, if ever, used)

Different Conduits for Tempting:

1. Visual
2. Verbal
3. Tactile

"Our next lesson will cover tempting a group. That will be the most challenging skill to learn. You must master the fundamentals before you're able to accomplish mass tempting. Make sure you're working toward that goal. I want all of you to succeed. And good luck out there today."

Artifice tramps his way into the heart of the pandemonium. He clears his throat and roars, "Welcome all, to the annual Tourney. Be strong and unrelenting. We will now be drawing names at random to select the five teams. Good luck."

When the names are called, I take my place next to nineteen strangers from the other Offerings. The corners of my mouth pull down as my teammates give last-minute hugs and kisses to their loved ones. There is no one in the stands rooting for me. No one will sing my praises if I win, and no one will comfort me when I surely lose.

We huddle up and the spectators cluster around the foreseers in the stands hoping for play-by-plays of their favorite players. My teammates bicker at once, arguing over game strategies. I keep quiet as they squabble over who should venture to other bases and who should stay behind to guard ours. A red-haired boy with pink skin gives me a wide-eyed glance before doing a double take. "Uh..." His forehead wrinkles. "Do you want to capture or defend?"

"Capture," I say.

"That settles it. The ten of you will scout for stones, and the ten of us will hang back defending ours," he says, gesturing with his hands. We line up at the entrance to our base and wait. A roll of thunder echoes, signaling the commencement of the game and we march through a partition in the wall of thorns. A sturdy stone pedestal awaits us on the other side, bearing a dazzling emerald.

The other scouts on my team immediately take off and disappear into the woods. I bend down and scoop some mud into my hands. I slather it over my face and neck until my skin is no longer visible. Maneuvering cautiously, I run from one tree covering to another. I trudge deep into the overgrown forest and strain my ears toward the far-off cries of other players.

The distant yelps are quickly overtaken by the heavy rustle of footsteps. A girl from a different team runs at full speed in my direction. I press myself up against the nearest tree, stilling my pounding heart. I stiffen as she closes in, but the girl zooms past me.

When I step out of hiding, a loud snap rings out from under my boot. The runner turns back to look, and I freeze. I close my eyes and hold my breath. But the girl marches onward in assertive strides. *Phew, that was close.*

My stomach flutters as I press on, hearing more commotion from a base up ahead. I creep from tree to tree. I lower myself onto my stomach at the top of a hill and peer down from behind a hedge of ferns. Hail showers the base, but a brave grower swings wildly through the pellets on a vine. A large chunk knocks him in the forehead, sending him straight to the ground. A red stream streaks down his face from the impact. I wince.

I push farther, hurdling over the uneven forest ground. Shouts and booms surround me, as I plunge deeper into the bush. I shove through the branches until I see another combat zone. This base is swarming, but most of the defenders are already engaged in tight scuffles. A healer mends a bloody gash on a boy's leg as he writhes in pain. Another defender has a girl pinned in a firm bear hug. "Let me go!" she screams.

The shiny ruby lies unblemished on its pedestal. But one unchallenged defender still circles the base. He has big hulking shoulders and grizzly arms. His fierce eyes dart through the woods to spot any would-be thieves. I poise to dash for the stone, waiting for the moment he turns his back.

Suddenly, Ruse rushes to strike from the other side. She stares him down and beelines fearlessly toward him. He shields his eyes and yells out a battle cry as he blindly charges her, tackling her to the ground.

As they wrestle for dominance, my right foot starts stinging. I look down to see that my boot has trampled on an ant bed, busy with ants scrambling to bite me. My foot thrashes violently in a panic. I yank off my boot as I hop away from the bed of ants, stabilizing myself on a nearby tree. As I whack my boot against the trunk, a sparkle catches my eye.

I lick my thumb and wipe away the grime from the shimmering bark, revealing a winning gemstone encased in the tree. My index finger traces the large opal stone as I read off the names of the winners:

Rose, Orchid, Petunia, Gale, Bolt,
Sibyl, Harbinger, Wily, Swindle, Vigor

Mother! I can't believe she never told me she won. I take a deep breath and step back into my boot. *You can do this.* I spy on Ruse as she finally makes stern eye contact with the guard. His body collapses on top of her, and he begins to snore loudly. She wiggles under him, but his dead weight pins her.

I dig my heels into the ground and dash to the base, snatching the stone from its haven. "You snake! That's mine!" Ruse shouts.

"Come and get it then." I run back toward my base with my eyes on the trees.

"She's got the stone!" Ruse screams. The other students abandon their fights, banding together to take me down.

"Give it up, girl! We're going to get you!" a boy shouts. I run as fast as I can, weaving between the woodland. A loud rumble echoes, and a young redwood tears through the earth to block the path just ahead of me. I dart left, but a tight patch of trees slows my pace. "Timber!" he yells. The roots snap, and the trunk topples toward me. I charge forward, barely missing a fatal squashing as the redwood slams down behind me.

My pursuers hurdle over the fallen tree, still hot on my trail. An electric bolt zips past me, instantly charring a bird in flight. The lifeless bird nosedives to the ground, showered by its feathers. "Really?!" *They said no deadly force!* My heart beats so fast that I am sure I will pass out, but I continue to crisscross between the trees still dodging more bolts.

I fish Storm's sapphire from my pocket, nearly dropping it as it slides against my sweaty palm. I tighten my grip and rub it, aiming behind me. The mighty blast of wind whooshes my rivals to the ground, bouncing them backward a couple of times after their initial impact.

I don't look back. My lungs burn and my legs ache, but I can finally see our base, overrun with enemies. I grit my teeth, clench the prized ruby, and keep plowing. A firm grip hooks my ankle, and I plunge face forward in a free fall. I toss the ruby overhead. "Catch!" I scream.

The red-headed boy snaps his head toward my call as the stone arches through the air. He dives for the stone, flopping onto his belly with a thud. He springs to his feet and victoriously places the ruby on the pedestal next to our emerald.

A deep, thunderous rumble resounds through the acreage. My teammates rush up from behind and scoop me onto their shoulders. They spin me around a few times in exuberant triumph. "You did it, you crazy girl!" the red-haired boy exclaims.

I raise my fists to the sky. "Woo-hoo!"

"Way to go, Jane!" Remedy shouts, jogging toward us from the woods.

"My plan actually worked," I call down to her.

All eyes shift to the Elders as they approach, dignified as usual. My team lowers me to the ground and stands by in respectful silence. "Congratulations to our team of winners. What an interesting turn of events in this ever-unpredictable game," Artifice says. He scrunches his nose at me, clearly put off by my sludge-smeared face. I stiffen as he leans in closer to halfheartedly pat me on the back. "Like mother, like daughter," he breathes.

Ginger peels back the thorn wall revealing the crowd of spectators with big smiles. The crowds leave the stands and gather around my team to celebrate their champions. We all watch as Ginger erects a large sycamore tree around the hefty ruby. Gust points at the stone with beams of scorching flares shooting from his fingertip, delicately engraving our names into the winning stone.

Fairmaster Beguile makes her way over to me. "Good job out there today." I wear a big smile surrounded by so many people and their compliments, but it grows much larger when I make out old Bud's figure off in the distance, leaning on his cane.

He hobbles toward me, and I excuse myself from all the attention to meet him midway. "Bud! You came!" I give him a gentle squeeze.

"Of course I did. Wouldn't have missed it for the world."

"Mother never told me that she won the Tourney. I saw her name out there."

He chuckles, waving his cane while he talks, "Right you are, young lady. Sibyl was never one to brag. But she won the Tourney single-handedly, just like you did today."

FOURTEEN

GAIN, I SIT ACROSS FROM Duplicity, looking into her contemptuous eyes. We've been at this since our return from winter break, squeezing in dozens of after-school tutoring sessions. All of them to no avail.

I never do much of anything except watch Duplicity showcase her Offering, having little influence over mine, which is in no rush to make its debut. I have learned nothing new except for my ever-growing distaste for my tutor.

We glare at one another, daring the other to blink first. Our gaze is broken by an unexpected knock at the door. A hard-faced Artifice nearly forces his way inside as I turn the knob. "Hello, Jane. How is your tutoring going?"

"Not well," I grumble as he follows me inside.

"Still no progress?" he asks in disbelief.

"No," Duplicity answers, disgust spoiling her face.

"I see. A word alone, please?"

"Of course," Duplicity says and joins him outside on my balcony.

They keep their voices low, so I can only make out every other word. I creep over to the window to listen better. "It's been months and there's been no change. That concerns me, Duplicity. I'm beginning to doubt if you're as reliable as I once thought," Artifice says.

"I've tried everything. It isn't my fault she can't do it. How can you blame me for that?"

"I needn't remind you the Trials are next month. No one, in the history of our kind, has *ever* had this kind of delay in their Offering. I refuse to have a tempter fail the Trials under my rule. I've entrusted this problem to you. If you want to succeed, take care of it." Every syllable he utters is reinforced by the severity in his eyes.

"I understand," Duplicity mutters.

"You have a week to produce some results. Or I will have to look elsewhere for my understudy." I rush back to my seat just before the door flies open and Duplicity storms back inside.

"Here's the deal, Jane. You're making me look bad. And I will not let you ruin my future. We're going to do drill after drill until you get it. Get up and follow me!"

I shadow her footsteps down the stairs and through the wilderness. "Where are we going?" I finally ask.

"Just pick up the pace. I don't have all day." Duplicity breaks into a jog, without even looking back at me. I grit my teeth as I try to match her pace. Before long, beads of sweat are blurring my vision. I rub my eyes to see Duplicity bouncing along with ease, barely perspiring. Just a sleek sheen—the kind that enhances the luster of naturally glowing skin. We run through the winding paths of the forest until she slows to a stop at the entrance to the Tourney grounds. I bend over to a squat, panting hard, as I brace myself against my knees.

"Now will you tell me what we're doing here?" I ask out of breath.

"I hope you're warmed up by now because, after every unsuccessful drill, you're going to run a lap around the Tourney field."

"You're kidding, right?" I say as the heat radiates from my face.

Duplicity rolls her eyes. "There's a sparrow on the limb of that pine. Secure eye contact and tempt the bird to raise both of its wings over its head. Snap, snap." I nod and creep closer. I stare at the shiny surface of the bird's eyes, holding a firm gaze for a few minutes. "Quit wasting my time and take a lap."

I bolt around the track. As I turn the corner on my way back around, Duplicity shouts, "The bird is still there. Try again." I catch my breath and give the bird another go, uniting our gaze once again. "Another lap!"

This time I come back wheezing. "AGAIN!" Still nothing. "You must be enjoying this. Take another lap!" I run six more laps before a cramp attacks my calf. My hair kinks tightly, soaking up my sweat like a sponge. "It's hopeless, but try again," Duplicity says with another eye roll.

My eyes are stinging, but I eyeball the bird as hard as I can. *This has to happen today. I am out of time.* The sparrow looks right at me but doesn't flinch. Just as I am about to give up, the bird makes a subtle movement. He stretches his left wing over his head. Then his right wing shoots up. "Whoa...are you seeing this?!" I ask, shaking with excitement.

"Sure took you long enough. Now we can finally go home," Duplicity replies flatly. I hop up and down, clapping my hands with joy while the sparrow relaxes his wings and returns to his natural posture. *I'm just a late bloomer!*

"While you get used to using your powers, it takes a lot out of you. And now that you *finally* have your Offering, we don't want to jinx it. I want you to conserve every ounce of power you have specifically for our sessions so that you can be ready for the Trials. Don't overexert yourself at home or in class."

"Thank you for helping me," I say, fanning my tears.

"Yeah, whatever."

FIFTEEN

I COAST THROUGH THE REST of the school year, what little is left of it. Everything is as it should've been all along. I may have been last-minute to come into my powers, but I swiftly wield them to their full extent.

"You all have come so far in this short year. The Trials are tomorrow, and I feel confident that you're all ready to pass. I cannot wait to see what you've prepared. It's been an honor to have you as students this year and I hope that I have impacted you all as much as you have me. Good luck tomorrow. And for the last time, class dismissed," Fairmaster Beguile says with a little curtsy.

"There's the birthday girl!" Remedy calls to me from the deck as I step onto the hanging bridge. She waits for me to cross and holds me at arm's length, looking me up and down. "Mm-hmm. Yep. You look older, alright. I knew I should've given you a healing stone to tend to those aching bones."

I frown. "Storm's bad sense of humor is rubbing off on you."

She rolls her eyes with a smile. "Very funny. I'll meet you at your place after I go home and change."

"Sounds good."

"See you soon, birthday girl!" She blows me a kiss.

Bud is propped up against his knotted, wooden cane waiting for me when I make it home. "Happy birthday, Jane! I have a very special gift for you." He hands over a rolled piece of parchment with a necklace wrapped around it. A chunk of raw diamond dangles from the thin, black rope.

"Wow. Thank you, Bud. But you really shouldn't have..."

"Oh, it's not from me. Your mother left it in my care to give to you on your eighteenth-year mark. I'll leave you to open it in privacy, but I hope you enjoy your day. If you ever need anything, you know my tree." Bud turns and hobbles off, careful to steady his cane before each step.

I step inside and take a seat in the living room with big eyes. My fingers tremble as I remove the necklace from around the parchment. I unravel the note and trace over each handwritten line with a delicate finger as I read:

My fairest Jane,

I'm so sorry I could not be there to wish you a happy birthday, but this will have to do. Always remember how much I love you. I could not be prouder of the woman you've become. In this stone, I have captured a vision for you. Use it in your time of greatest despair.

If you lose your way, follow the lion.

Warm tears spill from my eyes as I break down at Mother's loving words, leaping off the page and into my heart. "I miss you so much," I whisper, sobbing softly. I wipe my tears and ponder the words in the semi-cryptic note. "What do you mean, though?" I ask aloud, as if Mother will somehow respond.

"Jane, hurry up. We're going to be late," Remedy calls from outside.

"Just a minute, Rem." I slip the necklace over my head and open the door. Remedy is all smiles with her blond curls pulled back into low-hanging wolftails. She holds a small gift box out to me. "What do we have here?" I ask.

"Open it and see."

I slide the ribbon off and open the box. An opal stone glimmers inside. "A healing stone for my aching bones?"

"As promised."

I clutch the box with one hand and pull her in for a hug with my free arm. "Thank you."

"That's a beautiful necklace. Who got you that?" Remedy tugs at the necklace and pulls it closer to have a better look.

"Bud—er—my mother…It's a long story."

"It's stunning. Was there a vision inside?"

"There is…but I was instructed to wait for a particular time to view it."

"Ooh. Mystery. Your life is such an adventure, Jane."

"How do you figure? I'm as plain as they come."

"Don't be silly. The unheard-of delays in your powers, secret visions from your mother—after her death. Even your nonsensical name. You are many things, Jane, but ordinary is not one of them." *Huh. Never thought of it like that before.*

A shy smile pulls at my lips. "Maybe you're right."

"Of course I'm right. Now, come on. We don't want to be late." The low-hanging sun melts into evening and dusk slowly fills the sky. We cut through the forest to the path that leads down to the beaches. As we round the curved trail, a shaggy, dark-haired figure comes into view up ahead. "Storm!" Remedy calls after him.

Storm looks back at us and slows his pace. He greets Remedy with a quick peck on her cheek. "There you are," he says. His eyes find mine and he smiles. "Hey, Jane."

Other students trickle onto the path until it is flooded. I hear Duplicity's shrill laugh well before she rounds the corner some distance behind us, along with Augur and Ruse. I offer a friendly wave, which is not returned. I shrug and keep my pace with Storm and Remedy.

The sharp snap of a branch tugs my eyes to the woods, and I squint into the darkness. A pair of glowing eyes flash, as a massive, four-legged figure pounces onto the path before us. The nearby students scatter like roaches in a sudden shock of light. The cougar's yellow eyes lock onto a student just ahead of me.

"AHH!" the boy screams. The muscular shoulders of the monstrous cougar plow toward him. The boy quickly bends over and yanks on a small sprout protruding from the dirt. It shoots straight up, growing exponentially in size and height by the second. The boy clings firmly to a rising branch of the growing tree, farther and farther away from the cougar's reach.

The emergence of the tree slows the cougar some, but the animal jumps onto the large trunk after him. Its sharp claws tear into the tree as it heaves itself upward. The cougar climbs onto a sturdy branch, tail flicking, as it watches the boy climb higher with hungry eyes.

My heart falls through my chest and into my stomach. *Oh no! This must be the moment the foreseers predicted…And Mother always called them mountain lions instead of cougars! The note was confirmation!* "Hey! Over here!" I tremble as I shout.

"Are you crazy?! Don't call that thing over here!" Storm exclaims, holding Remedy tightly.

"Trust me, I got this. You two go hide."

"If you say so," he says, ducking behind some bushes with Remedy.

I wave my arms wildly and hurl a rock at the animal's backside. The cougar screams and jerks its head toward me with a snarl. It jumps down from the tree and closes in on me, hissing and growling with pure carnal instinct. I back up slowly and lock onto its hungry eyes. The cougar bares its sharp, carnivorous teeth.

Duplicity, Augur, and Ruse come running up behind us, but Ruse freezes in place at the sight of the cougar. A fearful gasp tears from her lungs. Nobody moves. The cougar stalks closer to me. A foamy drool oozes out of the sides of its mouth. I take another step back, but my foot gets caught on a root and I fall backward to the ground.

My anxiety soars but I spear the cat with my eyes. *You can't see me.* The cougar's face suddenly relaxes. Its whiskers twitch, and it drops its head to sniff around. With an explosive jump, the cougar launches over me, as if I were nothing but a small boulder in its way and disappears into the forest. I hold my face in my hands and exhale hard.

The young grower eases down from his tree. "You're a lifesaver! That was very brave of you to call that thing over your way. I was so scared…thank you," he says, still shaking.

"Really, Jane? Are you trying to get us all killed? What were you thinking, calling that furball over here like that?" Ruse says.

"I took care of it, didn't I?" I throw my arms up to reiterate my question.

"Barely! You just got your Offering! You got lucky!" Ruse huffs before storming off down the trail. Duplicity rolls her eyes and steps around me to cut ahead with Augur.

Storm and Remedy finally tiptoe out of the bushes. "Are you okay? Is it gone?" Remedy asks.

"Yeah, it's gone. It high-tailed it out of here faster than Storm did."

"Someone had to protect Remedy!" Storm snaps defensively.

"Yeah, yeah. You played a big role," I laugh.

Remedy steps forward to give me a tight embrace. "You saved us!" she says.

Storm steps in between us and wraps his arms around our shoulders. "Come on, you two. Now we have even more to celebrate. On to the bonfire!" The sky glows of faint pink and orange, where the sun has sunken into the sea, as we hike down the rocky hillside to the beach.

Near the shore, big rocks are arranged in a circle and Belladonna stretches her arms toward the center. Twigs expand and multiply with fury. They tangle and twist inward, outward, and on-to themselves in every direction. Storm steps forward and places his hand on top of the wood kindling, igniting a roaring fire. Everyone gathers around, brimming with excitement for the end of the school year.

"So, did you figure out what you're gonna do for the Trials tomorrow?" I hear the boy I saved from the cougar ask his friend. Remedy and I take a seat, sharing a large rock next to the two boys. The other boy places a finger to his chin in thought. He swishes his hand out in front of him, but nothing happens. He clears his throat and tries again, slower. A very brown and shriveled plant pains its way through the sand. It is so sad and wilted that I can't identify what kind of plant it is.

Remedy bends over the poor plant and closes her hand around the base of the shoot, transforming the stem to a vibrant green. Her supple fingers graze over the entire plant from base to bud. The leaves unfurl, and it grows larger until it blossoms into a stout and healthy sunflower. "If you could do that for me again tomorrow, that'd be great. I'm hoping I won't have to ask for volunteers from the audience to heal," Remedy says with her cheeks puffed, grinning from ear to ear.

"Are you nervous at all about tomorrow?" I ask her.

Her expression is pained. "I'd probably be less nervous coming face to face with a human!"

"You've been top of your class all year. Think about me. The girl who just got her Offering a month before the Trials. And for the record, humans aren't that scary. I've seen one!" I say, lowering my voice with a smile.

"No way! Did you see their yellow eyes? I heard they love the taste of Fairkind flesh. They grind up our bones and even use our teeth to make necklaces."

She makes me chuckle. "What? They don't have yellow eyes, as far as I could tell...I saw them after winter break. I skipped an extra day of class and visited Storm while he was patrolling the boundary. The day he gave me the sapphire to bring you for the Tourney. I thought I told you about it, but I guess I forgot."

"Are you sure they were humans? That doesn't sound like them."

"I'm pretty sure. Ask Storm. He was there, too."

"Oh, well, maybe the rumors aren't true," Remedy says, almost disappointed.

"We don't know for sure. Better safe than sorry, I guess," I say.

Storm sits down on the other side of Remedy. "And what are you two ladies giggling about over here?"

"The terrifying tales of humans!" I bare my teeth and chomp in Remedy's direction.

"Oh, so Jane told you how I fended them off?" Storm flexes his bicep and kisses it.

"No. We didn't get to that part," Remedy giggles.

"Let me tell you the heroic tale! But first, I almost forgot..." Storm says, standing to face the shore. He raises his hands, releasing bolts of voltage into the air. I duck instinctively, shoving my fingers inside my ears to drown out the cracks of thunder. When I look back up, Storm has scrawled out *"Happy 18th Birthday, Jane"* in his classic poor penmanship across the night sky.

"This is awesome!" I exclaim, hugging him as we watch the bolts of light fade.

Duplicity folds her arms, making sure her ring finger is visible. "This isn't a birthday party, Storm. Why don't you save that for afterward?"

"What's your problem, Duplicity? You have everything! Why do you try so hard to make everyone else miserable? Now that I have my Offering, you have no reason to torment me. I thought we could even be friends."

"Friends? Let me make this perfectly clear. You and I will never be friends. The only reason I even tutored you is because I am next in line to be an Elder, and rightly so. You were an annoying assignment, that's it."

Storm's face flushes crimson red, and his eyes burn. "How about you leave her alone?" he shouts angrily.

"Don't make me emasculate you right here in front of everyone," Duplicity snaps back. Her green eyes flicker, ready to lock him into a trance.

"Let's get out of here. We can find something better to do," Storm whispers defeatedly, backing down from Duplicity and leading us away.

"Yeah, maybe head to the Tavern with the old geezers. Happy birthday, Jane!" Duplicity says with an overdramatic wave.

SIXTEEN

*H*OOT. HOOT.

"**WHY TONIGHT?**" I shout, sitting up in my bed. The pestering owl's calls have kept me up half the night.

Hoot. Hoot.

I know I shouldn't waste my energy, but the Trials are today. And I really need a couple more hours of sleep. I wrap myself in a robe and storm onto my balcony. "Where are you, you feather-bag nuisance?" I call into the blackness. I spot the elusive owl perched on a branch, barely visible under the shadow of treetops. I breathe in deeply, filling my lungs with the crisp air of the wee morning hours. I hold it in for a moment before discharging it slowly, then lock my eyes on the tawny, brown owl. His lustrous golden eyes stare right back at me.

I need you to be quiet. I command him with my mind, eyeing him hard.

Hoot. Hoot.

"Owl: I want you to be silent. I command you, now. Silence!"

Hoot. Hoot.

"Ughh! Why isn't it working?"

I run back into the house and return with a teetering pot full of water. With all my might, I fling the water in the bird's direction. The unruffled owl remains dry as the water slaps the forest floor. I wind back my arm and hurl the pot over the balcony at him. We both watch as the pot arches up and then plummets down, with a hefty thwack on the ground below.

Hoot. Hoot.

Heavy footsteps sound from the darkness. I tremble as I peek over the railing. "Duplicity, what are you doing here? You scared me to death," I whisper.

"We need to talk."

"It couldn't wait until daylight?"

"Nope. Now, do you want to know why you couldn't tempt that owl?" I stare back at her, unable to speak. "Because you never got your Offering. I'm here to tell you that if you're dumb enough to go to the Trials today, you will fail. Maybe they'll hold you back a year and let you try again, but that's *never* happened before. It will send everyone into a panic."

I struggle to catch my breath as my heart flutters in my chest. "What are you talking about? You've seen me use it many times."

"Have you, though? Or have I been doing things for you, and letting you think it was you?"

"Wh-Why would you do that?" I stammer.

"Artifice gave me a deadline, Jane. What was I supposed to do? Have you ruin my life, too? I figured you'd eventually get it, so it wouldn't matter. But after the cougar incident, I knew we were out of time, and it just wasn't going to happen."

"Let me get this straight. You're saying that *you* tempted the cougar away?"

"Obviously."

I hang my head. "So, it only looked like I did it..." I say, realizing the vision Omen shared with me had been misinterpreted.

"No matter how you say it, it wasn't you."

I shiver. "You know, maybe—like you said—they'll let me retry next year."

"Do you honestly think that will change anything? That's never been needed before because that isn't the way of things. You don't have an Offering. You can't pull your weight around here and will only be a burden for everyone." I'm speechless as she continues, "Listen, now that Sibyl is gone you don't have any support here. Do you get that? You don't fit in and no one's going to help you."

"Don't you dare talk about her!"

"Just think about it. You drove your mother to her death because she always knew that you'd be a failure. If I were you, I would spare myself any more humiliation and run away to take my chances with the humans."

"I'm not going anywhere. And you're the one that will be humiliated when Artifice and the others find out about this little scheme of yours." My hands quiver with rage as my angry words cross my lips. "They won't even care that I don't have my powers because all scrutiny will be on you!"

Duplicity's eyes flare. "If that wasn't reason enough to leave, then this will be," she snickers. "Faking your Offering wasn't a waste after all because it has made me stronger in mine. Strong enough to see into the depths of your *father's* mind." Her words start to garble in my head as she emphasizes that word. "To see the shameful little secret that would ruin him—that he is the father of a nobody. Would you like to guess who that could be?" She folds her arms over her chest triumphantly as she waits for my answer.

"I don't believe you." My voice is hoarse and uneven, unconvincing.

A smirk rests on her lips. "Come on, Jane. It makes sense if you think about it. They worked together...poor Artifice. So sad."

"Why are you so cruel?!" I scream, unable to hold back my tears.

"The truth hurts. But my candor is doing you more favors than the saps out there who will coddle and lie to you," she says before disappearing back into the shadows.

I walk back inside and slam the door. Hot tears roll down as I drag into Mother's room and flop onto her bed. I stare at the knots in the wooden ceiling. "Artifice? How could you?" I blubber. I pull at my diamond necklace, still hanging around my neck. *Is this my time of greatest despair?* I fidget with the stone as I ponder. But before I decide, my eyes grow heavy, and my sobs finally give way to the deep sleep I have been seeking for hours.

SEVENTEEN

IJOLT AWAKE, REALIZING THE late hour. I've slept all day. Hours have passed since the Trials, and night covers the forest like a heavy blanket. My head still spins with lingering questions and emotions. I try to sort through them as I pace back and forth along the dusty hardwood floor of Mother's room. *I am the only Fairkind descendent to not receive an Offering—defective from birth—and worse still, abandoned by my own father in his pursuit of power.*

I cringe as I imagine the snickering faces of my peers when they hear the truth. *How can I ever face them again?* A still whisper of a thought slithers into my mind and grows until it reverberates into an indisputable truth: Duplicity is right. I do not belong.

Knock. Knock. Knock.

I freeze.

Knock. Knock. Knock.

"Open up, Jane. I can explain," says a low, stern voice. I do not want to answer the door, and certainly not for Artifice. But he owes me an explanation, and I intend on getting one. I fling the door open and stand there, indignant.

He stares at me blankly for a moment, searching my expression in the glow of his torchlight. He clicks his tongue before he starts, "You have every reason to hate me, but sometimes we must make sacrifices for the greater good. There was no one else fit to lead the tempters."

My eyes brim with tears as my throat tightens. "And who was fit to lead your daughter?"

"That's not fair. Sibyl didn't need me," he snaps, keeping his voice low.

"I needed you!" My scream startles me. He winces at my unabashed display of emotion, the torment in my eyes.

He scratches his head. "I did what I had to do. But I'm sorry you had to find out this way. Duplicity is not the leader I thought she was."

A scoff seeps from my lungs. "I think you should leave." His eyes darken to a cold, vacant stare. I can feel him watching my thoughts. Any other time I would be furious at the invasion, but I'm actually glad. He sees what my mouth fails to voice. The disgust and shame. How I want to speak of his relation to me even less than he does.

He stiffens under an arched brow and adjusts his cloak at the neck. "Well." He opens his mouth to say something else, but I slam the door in his face before he can continue. I wait there silently for minutes that seem like hours until I hear the tune of his footsteps walking away and down the steps. I creep to the window and quietly weep, watching my father's unaffected silhouette move farther away from me. *That's it. I need to go.*

I rush into my room and rummage through my dresser, shoving as many clothes as possible into my satchel. I dig through Mother's old writing desk until I find her Elder brooch, in the same drawer Herald had found it, and tuck it into a side pocket. I proceed into the kitchen to fill whatever room is left in my bag with food, a small knife, and the healing stone Remedy had given me. *Anywhere is better than here.*

I shut my eyes and take a deep breath. *I am leaving tonight.* I decide to sneak out of the back window in case Artifice is still watching. I secure my satchel on my back and heave up my right boot. Bracing each side of the window with my hands, I boost myself up and sit on the ledge. My heart races as my feet dangle, hovering over the nothingness. A faulty landing could easily leave me with broken bones.

I take a deep breath and hold onto my necklace, looking back to steal one last look around my house. *Mother, please help me.* Plunging feet first, I push out toward the ground. I land hard but tuck headfirst into a tumbling roll. I scramble to my feet and take off as quietly as I can, staying far from the main paths.

I hike through the moonlit forest for the rest of the night and stop to rest in a small cave just as the darkness starts to lift. After sleeping a few hours, I continue onward toward the border. According to Storm, it will take at least a couple of days to get there so I collect any berries and nuts I come across and drink from streams.

After shoving through the uncut forest for two more days, I finally reach the border at dusk. I fish out my measly knife and cut into the thicket. Before even putting a dent in it, footsteps approach along the wall. I crouch low to the ground, hoping the darkness will be enough to hide me.

The figure extends his hand and exposes me with a high beam of light from his palm. "Jane! We've been so worried about you. Are you okay?"

I stare at Storm dumbfounded, blinded by his light. His palm returns to its normal opaque state, and he smooths it over the stubble on his cheek uncomfortably. "That was a dumb question. Of course you're not okay," he says, holding out his other hand to help me up. I want to say something, but no words come.

He senses my shortcoming and fills the silence. "Um, Duplic-ity told everyone that Artifice is your father," he blurts, and I can feel the immediate heat in my cheeks as they begin to burn. "...But the good news is that he has been stripped of all his power." My eyes enlarge. "Yep. He's done for. Duplicity tried her best to gar-ner support for his vacant seat but that didn't go over too well with the other Elders. They won't even entertain the idea."

"It doesn't matter," I finally mutter. "I never got my powers, Storm. I have nothing left here and I'm leaving." I turn back to cut at the thicket again.

"Jane, please, you don't have to do this. This will all blow over. It's dangerous beyond these walls."

"My mind is made up. Either help me or leave me alone," I snap. Storm shakes his head and cups his hands around his mouth. A white, wispy fog propels from his parted lips and swirls around as it thickens. He blows the billowing cloud up against me, and I fall backward onto the condensed bed of air.

"Good luck, Jane. I hope you find some peace beyond our world. You deserve it," he says as the cloud carries me over the boundary line.

"I'll miss you and Rem," I call back to him as I jump off a few feet from the ground, just clearing the end of the thicket.

EIGHTEEN

THE GROUND UNDER MY FEET is rough and bumpy as I trudge for hours through the dark wilderness. Exhaustion sets in, but I plow forward. My left boot skids over a patch of dry leaves and I lose my footing. I had unknowingly been inching closer to the edge of a steep slope. Down the hill I tumble, until I am dumped into the arms of a rushing river.

My garbled screams are silenced by the water as I plunge beneath the surface. The swift current whisks me downstream while I thrash my way back up for air. My lungs draw in a deep breath when my head surfaces, but the cold choppy waters force me down again. I throw my arms up and heave myself above the water. *I haven't made it this far to drown in a rotten river.* I paddle across and out of the hostile current. Reaching the refuge of the bank, I lie there, face down in the muck as the rough waters lap against my legs.

A pitiful cry escapes me as I clench the damp, rooted ground. I am chilled to the bone. *Mother, I need you.* I grab my necklace. It hasn't been lost to the force of the river. A surge of hope. My trembling fingers rub the stone.

The diamond glows and a foggy haze swirls inside. I squint while the image forms. When the smoke clears, a starry night sky comes into focus. Nine stars shine brighter than the rest, forming the distinct shape of a wildcat. "Follow the lion," I say aloud, remembering Mother's words in the note. *Oh, I get it now.*

My eyes rise to the sky above the river. I hold up the stone, comparing the stars in the sky to the image. I clamber to my feet and hobble in a circle. There it is. The twinkle of a star-studded lion. I check the stone a final time, just before the vision fizzles out and the diamond returns to its natural translucent state. *I trust you, Mother.*

I follow the constellation until nearly dawn, finally emerging from the forest. I pause, encountering a strange black path stretching across the vast horizon. It feels firm underfoot, so I walk along the odd path toward the sun peeking over the trees in the distance. My clothes are still damp, but the rising sun is warm on my skin.

After a while, I hear a faint humming from behind. I search anxiously as the noise drones on but see nothing. I sprint farther down the winding path, fearful of that which makes the sound. The noise grows nearer, still, until I am running at full speed. *HONK. HONK.*

I whip my head back to see a large red beast bearing down on me. I dive straight into a ditch and hunch myself low. The beast screeches to a halt, and I peek up from the ground. I watch wide-eyed as a door swings open.

My heart nearly stops beating as a human hops out. His gray hair is scraggly, and an untamed beard grows down to his collar. "What were ya thinking, running in the middle of the road like that?!" the scruffy human asks me. The hair around the edges of his mouth is stained a pale yellow and his voice carries a bizarre twang.

I jump to my feet, knees shaking. "I'm so sorry. Please don't hurt me."

He chuckles. "Oh, honey, I'm not gonna hurt ya! I was just going to offer you a ride. We're quite a ways from civilization out here."

"I-I'm fine, really. Thank you anyway," I stutter, taking a guarded stance.

He frowns as he surveys my disheveled appearance. "I can't just leave you out here in the middle of nowhere…it's dangerous. At least let me take you into town and buy you a hot meal," he says, extending his arm out to me. The massive tank that almost flattened me still hums softly.

I search the man's eyes for any trace of malice but find only sincerity. I reach for his thick, callused hand and allow him to pull me out of the ditch. "Thank you," I reply, keeping my voice steady. *There's no turning back now.*

"You're very welcome," he says, opening a door on the other side of his beast for me. I climb inside, trying my best to remain calm. The man jumps in on the other side and sits behind a large wheel. His pants are fastened over his shoulders by two black straps with a white T-shirt underneath.

With two fingers, he lifts a white stick to his lips and lights the end on fire. Smoke puffs from his mouth as the end of the stick burns bright orange. I stifle a cough as the air grows thick inside the cabin of his beast. "Does this bother you? Sorry. Where are my manners?" he says, flicking the stick out of his window.

"Oh, that's okay. You didn't have to do that."

"The missus would kill me if she found out anyway. I've given up the nasty habit, but it's been a very long drive, you see. Name's Chuck. Pleased to meet ya," he says, revealing a charming smile.

I force a smile, hoping he can't sense my fear. "I'm Jane…"

"You scared the bejesus outta me," he says with a small chuckle. "Where might ya be headed? Have ya been on foot long?"

I pause, unsure of what to say. "No. Just a couple days." The silence is palpable as he views me with curious eyes. I can tell he wants to question me further but remains quiet.

"That's mighty brave of ya," he finally says. "I haven't been out this way in a long time, young lady. I got a good deal on a few parts for my tractor at a farm down here. Now I'm headed home to my ranch in Washington. But my next stop is Portland, to grab a bite and refuel for the last leg of my trip."

I let out a big yawn. My eyes are suddenly heavy. "You look sleepy," he says. "Why don't you go ahead and take a nap? Here, you can use my jacket as a pillow." He hands over an old black leather jacket, which has the same lingering fetor as his burning stick. "That there's my old biker jacket. It's seen better days, but it's soft." *This human doesn't seem so bad.*

"Thank you." I fold up the jacket and put it under my head as I lean against the door.

Hours later, the constant stop-and-go of the beast jars me from my slumber. "Rise and shine. We're here," Chuck says. Beyond the busy black path, odd buildings disappear into the clouds. They cluster tighter than the redwoods of the forest. Trees are sparse, looking hardly sturdy enough to hold their own branches. Even the few leaves are yellowed and drooping. Horns honk and metal beasts zip around and between each other like rapids gushing around jutted rocks. I'm not sure where everyone is going, but they are all in a very big hurry to get there.

I stretch my arms as he steers the beast under the shade of a large awning. He hops outside and races around to open my door. "You're going to love Mama Betsy's. This truck stop's a little-known secret, but they got the best biscuits and gravy within a hundred square miles. Breakfast is my treat." I step out and inhale deeply. A bitter filth weighs the air, giving me a taste of impurities with each breath. I scrunch my nose. "Everything alright, darling?"

The sharp pong ignites in my nostrils and burns all the way down to my lungs. "What is that awful smell?"

"The diesel you mean? Yessiree. How else would I power this beauty?" Chuck says, patting the hood of his beast. "Come on, you must be famished. I'll fill 'er up afterward."

I nod and follow him. The smell doesn't seem to bother anyone else, especially not the number of men with lined faces pouring out from "Mama Betsy's" in droves. They are followed by a robust aroma that cuts through the stench in the air. The door they exited from opens again with the chime of a bell, and another wave of delicious scents rolls into my nostrils.

Chuck holds the door open for me as I step inside the place of wondrous smells. He takes a seat at a table and gestures for me to sit across from him. An aged lady with thin red lips saunters to our table within a minute. Her hair is in a bun, and a white apron hugs her waist. "It's good to see you again, Chuck. And who might you be?" The woman looks directly at me.

"This is my new friend, Miss Jane," Chuck answers for me. I give an uneasy smile as the woman takes me in.

Her nostrils flare ever so slightly, noting my apparent stench. After a moment, she quickly sets her face into a proper smile. "What can I get you, folks? Our special today is biscuits and gravy with a side of bacon and eggs."

Chuck clears his throat. "Sounds good to me, Martha. And an orange juice, please. What would you like, Jane?" I read the woman's nametag slowly in my head. *M-A-R-T-H-A. Chuck and Martha. Such odd names—odd names like Jane.*

"Ma'am?" Martha snaps in her raspy voice.

"Oh, yes. I'll have the same thing, please."

"Great choice. I can tell we're going to get along just fine, you and me." Chuck's eyes are bright as he says this, and for some reason I can't quite explain I begin to relax in his presence. I glance around at the other humans nearby, observing them carefully,

studying their speech, and—more importantly—their movements. But I am happy to find that they are completely oblivious
of me.

The chatter becomes barely audible under the whir and
sputter of a massive silver machine pouring brown liquids into
mugs. The dull roar of pressurized hissing convinces me something is due to explode at any moment, but Martha braves the
fancy equipment, operating it without batting an eye. She presses
a button, and a bin of black beans attached to it spins madly,
crunching and grinding away.

The cheeks of a girl at a neighboring table are impaled with
metal balls where dimples should be. A small hoop pierces her
right eyebrow. Colorful pictures swath her exposed skin and
random phrases are scrawled on her forearms. The girl catches me
gazing too long and glowers back with an equally disturbed look.
She seems just as horrified by my underwhelming appearance. I
tremble and look away.

Many of the humans hold odd devices to their ears and
gossip into them. It is the strangest thing to see humans in full-
blown conversations with an object. Some humans are tall, some
are short—some thin, some hefty. Their clothing and mannerisms
vary significantly from person to person. They bear few similar-
ities, other than their humanity.

Martha returns shortly with a steaming plate in each hand
and plops them on the table. I look down with skeptical eyes,
poking at the strange slop with my fork. "Eat up, now, before it
gets cold," Chuck insists. I close my eyes and hesitantly take a
small bite. My eyes shoot open, as my palate explodes with new
flavors. *Delicious!* I inhale the strange food, only looking up to
notice that Chuck is not even halfway finished as I scarf down my
last few bites. "My, my, you were hungry," he laughs. I dab my
mouth with a napkin and flash a sheepish smile.

After Chuck finishes his plate and gulps down the rest of his orange juice, Martha comes back with a piece of parchment and places it in front of him. He hands her some green slips from his pocket. "That should cover it. Keep the change." We walk out of the truck stop together with satisfied bellies. "Well, this is my last stop before heading back to my ranch. What's your plan?"

I look down. "I'm just going to take it day by day," I say, fidgeting uncomfortably. I look back up to see his face etched with concern.

"Jane—and I hope I'm not overstepping here—but I could use an extra set of hands with the animals on the ranch. And I have a room to put you up in until you get on your feet. It's not much but it's cozy."

"Wow. That's very generous of you but…"

"You say generous, I say kismet. I need help and, please don't take this the wrong way, but I believe you do too."

My ears perk up. I seldom hear the use of that word, and only by Mother until now. "Yes, it must be kismet." I smile. "And thank you for everything, Chuck."

NINETEEN

WE ROUND THE BEND TO the ranch in just inside of two hours. Chuck presses something on his door and my window lowers into the beast. A soft breeze caresses my face as we coast down the long dirt path. He cracks a smile. "Welcome to our ranch. Right in the fearsome underbelly of Mount Saint Helens."

A large sign saying, "*Anselmo Ranch*" greets us under a backdrop of snowcapped, rolling mountains. Bright green pastures span the distance beneath the range. "It's greener than any emerald," I say in awe. He nods, smiling to himself as he steers the beast down the path. Massive black and white creatures I've never seen before dot the vast greens.

Chuck follows my gaze. "You can't have any green without a little brown, am I right?"

I'm confused. "Come again?"

"Those heifers provide a lot of manure and then some. Don't worry, you'll see soon enough." About that time, a sleek curvy animal with long legs and flowing black hair gallops alongside the beast. "Let's see what ya got, ya ole Boots," Chuck says, tightening his grip on the wheel. My heart quickens in my chest as we speed up, racing the majestic creature called "Boots".

Boots beats us by a landslide. Chuck guffaws as we roll to a stop, watching the animal rear back on its hind legs in triumph. A young man runs up from behind the creature, twirling a long rope overhead. When he lets it go, a loop slides perfectly around Boots' neck. Chuck comes around to open my door and I step outside. "Sorry, Dad. Boots got out again. We need to repair that paddock gate before it gets dark," the young man says, panting hard. He is tall and striking.

He wipes the beads of sweat from his forehead with the back of his hand. His bicep bulges with the movement, cuffed by a plain white T-shirt. I skim over his pronounced shoulders until my eyes meet his squared jawline. The tips of his dark hair are wet under a big hat as he shakes his head to the side to move the hair from his eyes. His dark eyelashes are full, and he carries a tiny scar through his left eyebrow. I feel my heart beating. *So fast...*

"JANE!" Chuck shouts, gently shaking my shoulder. "I said I'd like you to meet my son, Michael." The young man looks a tad smug, having caught me staring at him so closely. "Jane will be staying with us for a while," Chuck adds.

Chuck's son walks closer to me with his hand out. "Just Mike is fine." His sea-green eyes suck me in like an undertow. I get lost in them for a full moment before realizing he's waiting on me. I jerk my hand into his, not entirely certain this is what he is expecting from me. His hand is worn but comforting as he gives my palm a gentle shake.

I offer him a shy smile and whisper, "Jane."

He grins. "It's nice to have a fresh face around here. Well, if you'll excuse me, I need to return Boots, here, back to the stables." He tips his cream-colored hat down a smidge with his thumb and index finger. He lifts it once more. "Ma'am," he says in a polite tone. Then he walks off, leading Boots away.

"Alright, young lady, let's get you squared away." Chuck pats me softly on the back, guiding me in the direction of their house. It sits directly on the ground, like the buildings I saw earlier. *Things are very different here.* It is a fine home with a wraparound porch, rocking chairs, and a hanging bench, creaking as it swings in the breeze.

Chuck scoops a handful of seeds from a bucket on the porch and flings them to the ground. In the blink of an eye, we are surrounded by a dozen birds on foot, pecking furiously at the handout. As they cluck at each other, I wonder when they will get spooked and fly off, but they never do. "What's wrong with them?" I ask.

"Bertha quit laying eggs a few days ago, so I'm not too pleased with her." Chuck side-eyes one of the odd birds.

"Can they not fly, I mean?"

"Of course not. These, here, are chickens."

"So, then why do they have wings?"

"You know, that's an excellent question. I couldn't tell ya." His belly jiggles as he hoots with laughter. He leads me inside and shows me around their lovely, big home. My room is cozy, as promised, with a big bed and dresser drawers. The large window features a view of the summit, capped with a glistening frost.

"I'll let you get settled. The shower is right next door if you would like to freshen up. There's towels and soap in there for you. And Mrs. Anselmo serves supper at five o'clock sharp," Chuck says and shuts the door, leaving me to myself.

I raise an arm over my head and quietly sniff my underarm. The smell is pungent, and I'm suddenly overcome with gratitude for Chuck's hospitality. *I wouldn't have made it far had it not been for the kindness of this human.* My eyes moisten at the thought.

After fumbling my way through my very first shower, a fresh pair of clothes waits for me on my bed. They're a little snug but will do just fine. A bell chimes throughout the home at the top of every hour. When I hear its chirping as evening falls, I hurry into the dining room Chuck pointed out to me earlier.

A round woman bustles back and forth, setting platters of food on the table. She lets out a tired sigh and brushes the hair back from her face. She wipes her hands on her apron and marches around the table to better examine me. "You must be Miss Jane! I hope you're hungry. I've made quite a meal in your honor." Her eyes shine atop an easy smile.

"I see you've already met the missus," Chuck says as he enters the room. He shuffles behind us and takes a seat at the head of the table.

"Please—call me Mabel." I nod politely as she takes a seat across from Chuck. "Go ahead, dear," she urges, gesturing to the seat on her left. I sit down and stare blankly at the empty place setting in front of me, secretly wondering when Mike will arrive. Then the screen door slams and my entire body tenses. *Here he comes.*

He traipses in and practically collapses into the vacant chair. "What a day," he breathes in exasperation. "But Secretariat himself couldn't buck his way out of that gate now."

Chuck claps his son proudly on the back. "Nice work, my boy!"

Two furry animals followed Mike inside, presently nipping at his heels. Their coats are mostly black, but their chests are white. The uncanny resemblance they share with wolves frightens me.

Their claws rap against the hardwood floor, dragging themselves closer to me to take in my scent. *No! Stay back!!* They sniff my legs, and I jerk my feet away in fear. One of them growls at me softly, undoubtedly aware of my distinct differences from my hosts. I cower instinctively until I am visibly shrinking into my chair. "Oh, hush up, Cooper! He's just old and grumpy. They won't bite you," Chuck says matter-of-factly.

"Michael Wayne Anselmo! I have told you to keep those dogs out of my dining room on more than one occasion!" Mabel booms.

Mike's face falls. "But they're family, Ma."

"Oh, for Heaven's sake," she fires back, rolling her eyes. "I better not find a single strand of dog hair on my plate, and I mean it." She shakes her head and turns to me, handing me a heaping plate of food. "So, Jane, do you hail from these parts?"

"Um…" Suddenly the room is warm and stuffy. *What do I say here?* My feet fidget uncomfortably under the table. I can't find my voice, and everything goes out of focus except for a glimpse of Mike, secretly slipping scraps of food under the table to his terrifying animals.

Chuck clears his throat a little too loud and exchanges a look with Mabel. "How long did ya say that gate took ya, son?" he asks, abruptly turning to face Mike and I'm so grateful for the change of subject. Mike proceeds to detail the arduous process of repairing the fence for the next twenty minutes. Well, I can't be sure that was all he went over. It is hard to focus on anything while gazing into his mesmerizing eyes. I can hardly look away.

As our plates empty, Mabel excuses herself to clear the table. I offer to help but she graciously refuses. "You go on and relax for the evening. Ranch life calls for early days, and I want you to be well-rested in the morning," she explains.

"Thank you very much for dinner. The food was wonderful," I say, trying to suck in my bloated belly as I rise to stand. My heart hammers as I squeeze behind Mike's chair to exit the dining room.

"Goodnight, Jane," he calls after me.

I look back to take him in once more. "Goodnight," I whimper, hating myself for allowing a mere human to have this kind of effect on me. I head straight to my room and sink under the covers, hoping they hadn't heard the click of my door locking. *Can't be too careful.*

My window frames the night sky in its star-studded glory all from the comfort of my bed. I rub my tired eyes and turn over to catch a glimpse of Mother's lion watching over me. I cradle my necklace and doze off into a peaceful slumber.

TWENTY

I AM AWAKENED BY A shrill scream. I can still see the stars through the darkness, although fainter now. Before I can even get my bearings, another scream cries out and I jump to my feet. *What could that be?!* I panic inwardly, the sound of the shrieking reminding me how foreign the land of humans is, how many dangers I have yet to encounter.

I am scared to look, but I tiptoe to the side of the window and peer out into the darkness. On the ground, I see a fat bird like the chickens I met yesterday, but this one has a red flame engulfing his head and a beard to match. My fears subside instantly, and I breathe out a sigh of relief.

The others must have heard the screeching too, because I hear their soft stirrings. I drag myself into the bathroom and flip the switch to initiate the light like I had seen the others do the night before. I jump back, frightened by the person looking back at me from over the basin. *Oh, right. This is going to take some getting used to.* I've seen my reflection in rivers and streams before, but never this exact. My long, brown hair has that messy slept-in look and a dark hue rests underneath my eyes.

My hosts have left me a small brush next to a tube labeled "toothpaste". I open the tube and take a whiff. *Minty.* Back home, it is customary to clean one's mouth by swishing water throughout the day and chewing mint leaves for fresh breath. I shrug and squirt a little paste on the brush, hesitantly inserting it into my mouth. I gently move the brush back and forth across my teeth. When the white foam turns red, I quickly spit to discover that my gums are bleeding. *Maybe more gentle next time?*

I rinse my mouth until it runs clear again and dash from the bathroom, ready to leave the magic water supply and reflective glass behind. As I exit, I am startled by a shirtless Mike leaning casually against the wall. His hair is tousled from sleep. My eyes move over his defined chest and each perfect bump of his abdomen.

"Good morning," he says in a husky voice, shooting me a gorgeous half-smile. *Oh wow.*

"Good morning to you," I say, prying my eyes from his well-sculpted body to look down at my feet.

"Breakfast is almost ready. Be sure to eat up because we've got a busy day ahead of us. I'll show you how we milk the cows later this morning," he says before strolling into the bathroom and subsequently parting us with a door.

I make my way to the dining room where Chuck is already sipping from a mug, reading an extra-long parchment. His eyes light up as he glances at me. He folds his parchment and lays it on the table beside him. "How did you sleep, my dear?"

As I ponder his question, I realize it was one of the best sleeps I have ever experienced. The heavy, warm blanket lulled me into a sound slumber only interrupted by the screech of the fiery fowl. "I slept great. Thank you again for your hospitality."

"It's our pleasure. We're excited to have you join our crew!" he exclaims. After a beat, Mabel comes barging in bearing trays of eggs, sizzling meats, and breakfast pastries. The smells compete for dominance in my nostrils, as I debate which foods I will taste first. I can't help but lick my lips as I sniff the crispy strips of meat. *What Mabel serves tastes so much better than the wild game of the forest.*

"Smells good, Mom." Mike verbalizes my thoughts, entering the dining room with a fresh white T-shirt and stiff blue pants. He takes his seat across from me.

"Eat as much as you want. There's plenty to go around," Mabel says.

"Yes, ma'am," he replies before taking a bite out of a pastry. I watch a crumb cling to his bottom lip before he licks it away.

"Jane, have you ever worked with animals before?" Mabel asks, breaking my stare from her son.

"No, *ma'am*," I say, mimicking Mike's vernacular. "Not really, but I have always been fond of them." I smile as the memory of me launching a pot at the hooting owl flickers in my mind.

After we've eaten, Mabel offers me some fresh clothes called "overalls" to change into, and I make haste to begin my day. Chuck gives me a tour of the ranch including the henhouse, pig pens, barn, and family garden. "Hay and wheat are big cash crops up here in Washington, so we grow plenty of that. Good way to make some extra cash and we use as much as we need to care for the horses. We can make a quick buck off the dairy too," Chuck explains. "But the chickens, pigs, and our other crops are just to keep food on the table 'round here. The missus hates going into town, you see." I continue to follow him around to the other side of the ranch, trying my best to commit everything he says to memory.

Soon, a beautiful wooden building materializes before my eyes, only outshone by the green lawn that surrounds it. "Here we have the stables and pasture, and the corral is out back, behind the stables."

My jaw hangs agape as Boots and others of his kind gallop into view. I count seven of them—pure black, chestnut brown, white with brown splotches, white with black speckles, white with brown speckles, pure white, and gray. Chuck clicks his tongue. "Magnificent animals, horses are," he says in wonderment.

"They're so…regal," I agree. "They're all yours?"

"Boots and Buster are." He points to the black and chestnut brown ones. "The others are here for training."

"What kind of training?"

"Training for competitive equestrian events—dressage and show jumping. Things of that sort."

"Oh wow, I didn't know you trained animals."

"Mercy me, I don't train them. No, I leave that to Walter's expertise. You'll meet him here soon. Come now, these cows won't milk themselves, unfortunately." I follow him back across the pasture until we reach the red barn again. Mike is already inside, seated on a stool squeezing the underside of one of the cows by hand. I hover over him, watching his movements closely as he milks her.

"Here, give it a try," he says and gives up his stool for me.

I am nervous as I take a seat. "You're sure it's safe?"

He chuckles. "Of course. Why wouldn't it be?" *Because she's big enough to down me in one swallow?*

"You can't be too careful," I say. "So, I just tug on the nipple?"

Mike exchanges a quick laugh with Chuck. "Not exactly." He kneels beside me, so his face is but a breath away from mine. "These are the teats, and this entire area is her udder," he explains, gently washing some dirt off her underside. He drags a bucket under the area. My heart throbs as he places his hand over mine and guides it around the top of the teat. "Gently pinch it at the top and then use your other fingers to apply more pressure." My fingers imitate his, as they rest against mine. I gently grip the teat and squeeze until a stream of milky white cream shoots into the bucket.

"I did it!"

"Yes, you did," Mike says with a laugh. "Only a hundred more squeezes to go." My eyes bulge when I hear the number and Mike must have noticed because he follows up with, "But don't worry, you're a natural. I'll go get Cooper and Ace to herd the other cows in and we can knock this out together." I smile and nod, then Mike turns and heads outside, whistling for the dogs.

"If you need anything, I'll be in the stables, watering the horses," Chuck tells me, before leaving in the opposite direction. I continue to milk the cow, filling up the pail about halfway before Mike leads another cow inside the barn. He takes a seat next to me and begins to milk his cow. Only the spray of the milk against the tin buckets fills the silence. My heart flutters as I rack my mind for something to say. *Come on. There's got to be something interesting I can talk about.*

"I—," I start to say.

"So—," He cuts me off. We both giggle. "You go ahead," Mike insists.

"I was just going to say that I really like your family."

"Yeah, they're pretty great."

"What were you going to say?" I ask.

He reddens and sweeps his hair back from his face. "I was just wondering how old you are. We look around the same age."

"Oh, I just turned eighteen. How old are you?"

"Twenty," he says. Another silence spans between us. I want nothing more than to get to know this beautiful human, but my mind draws a blank. My heart leaps when he speaks again. "I know my parents are happy to have you here. We lost my sister to meningitis a few years ago and there's been a void in our family ever since. She would have been nineteen now." *Meningitis? Sounds scary.*

"I'm so sorry to hear that," I say, placing a reassuring hand on his arm. He glances up at me with hope in his eyes.

After a moment, I reluctantly retract my hand. "I also lost a loved one," I say, looking down. "My mother passed last year. I know how painful it can be."

Mike doesn't reply but looks at me intently and squeezes my hand. I get lost in his stare for what feels like forever. I breathe in his woodsy scent and feel instantly at home.

"Ahem," a low growl cuts in. Mike immediately withdraws his hand, and we fix our eyes on a human with a stance as rigid as the fitted clothes he wears. His hair looks slick and pasted to his head. A crisp, white-collared shirt is tucked neatly into his tight slacks. A black belt circles his waist needlessly—his pants are in no danger of falling. Shiny, knee-high boots cleave to his legs, and he carries an ominous black stick tucked under one arm.

"Morning, Walter," Mike says.

"Mike," Walter replies curtly. "The new help I take it?" he asks, looking down his nose at me. *Who does this guy think he is?*

I glance at Mike who says, "This is Jane. A pleasant addition to our crew."

"I see. Well, I hate to interrupt such a tender moment…"

"Oh, not at all." Mike brushes our moment off a little too quickly. My spirit sinks. *It was a tender moment…*

"Billy didn't muck out the stalls and they're filthy. Would you be able to take care of that? Or perhaps Jane, here, could?"

"Sure, I'll get right on it," Mike says.

Mike bustles out of the barn and Walter stalks closer until his shadow eclipses me. "I oversee the stables around here…So far, I've trained three Olympic horses who won the gold in equestrian events. You've probably heard of me—Walter Greene?" He looks at me expectantly.

"I'm sorry, I haven't. But I'm new to the area. That all sounds wonderful, though, really," I offer, without a clue as to what he's talking about.

"In other words," he bends at the waist, so we are eye-to-eye, "I call the shots around here. And you better believe if you aren't a good fit, I will be the first to let you know." The hostility in his voice assures me that he means to make good on this threat.

I look at him expressionless, unsure of how to respond. I nervously turn back to milking. "Well, Jane, I'll let you get back to your little toiling." He whips his black stick over his shoulder and begins to walk off but turns back after a few steps. "By the way, your technique is all wrong," he adds before leaving the barn. *I need to keep my eye on that one.*

TWENTY-ONE

I WAKE BEFORE THE CROW of the rooster—that's what they call him—eager for my day of training at the horse stables. I fill up on a hearty breakfast and waste no time in getting there. Mike and another young man I have yet to meet are waiting for me inside. Behind them, a wall of shiny plaques and ribbons glints in the soft light of dawn.

"Jane, this is Billy, another one of our farmhands," Mike says.

Billy is just shy of Mike's generous stature. His dirty blond hair is cropped short, and his groggy brown eyes struggle to meet mine. "Morning," he yawns.

"Okay, first order of business for today, we will turn the horses out and that will give us a chance to muck out the stalls, then we can fork more hay into their nets, and refill their troughs. Jane, follow Billy down to the opposite end and he will show you how we turn them out," Mike directs.

Several of the horses are keen on his plan, already poking their heads enthusiastically from their stalls. As Billy and I enter the stall farthest back, I watch him lift each leg of the horse to methodically inspect the soles of its feet. "I'm doing a quick check of his legs, hooves, and shoes. This must be done before each horse is turned out," he informs me.

The horse rotates his elongated head toward me and snorts playfully. I hesitantly reach out and touch his velvet nose and he nuzzles my palm. "Jane, try to stay focused," Billy grumbles with a glare.

"Sorry," I say, feeling stupid and redirecting my attention to his demonstration.

"All clear." He unhinges the gate on the stall, pats the horse above his tail, and the horse trots out of the stables. We repeat the process until we have released all the horses into the pasture.

A sarcastic smile splits Mike's face as he approaches me and Billy saying, "Now for the fun part: mucking out the stalls." Billy cackles dramatically, and I have an immediate aversion to him. "Oh, come on. It's not that bad. Plus, now there's three of us." Mike's eyes light up as he casts his stare on me. I smile briefly and look away, trying not to display my desire for his attention.

It takes three grueling hours to thoroughly clean out the stalls, and if my partners are any indication of how I look, I don't want to see. They are covered in stinky "manure", sweat, and bits of straw. *I can't believe I looked forward to this*. I wipe my brow with the back of my forearm, despite the aching pain, and exhale slowly. My arms are useless to me now, just as Walter's belt is to his pants.

We round the horses up and return them to their stalls. Only one stall remains empty as I walk to the front where Mike and Billy stand. "Where's the white one?" I ask with concern.

"That would be Milady, Carla's horse. She is riding her out back in the paddock. Still trying to break her in actually—$15,000 for a purebred Arabian that still manages to clip the shortest of jumps. But she'll learn," Mike says, nodding his head with certainty, "Walter will see to that." He cracks an imaginary whip at me.

"Yes, now that you mention it, is that normal practice for Walter? To use a whip on the animals, I mean?"

Mike shrugs. "Anyone serious about the sport uses a riding crop. But he tends to be a little heavy-handed at times, I'll admit."

"Oh, okay. I'm still new to all this so I wasn't sure."

"Would you like to see them practice?"

"Yes!"

He smiles at my overzealous response. "You coming, Billy?"

"Nah. You've seen it once, you've seen it a thousand times," Billy answers, rolling his eyes.

Mike nods and places a light hand on the small of my back, guiding me toward the paddock. "Right this way," he says. We exit the stables just as a beautiful young woman sails over a hurdle on the back of the pristine white horse. "Well, she cleared that," he says with surprise. My heart sinks when he drops his hand from my back to lean against the railing and look at the rider.

Her sleek, blond braid falls perfectly down her back as they touch down on the other side. I watch in envy as she rounds the course several times, clearing all but the final jump. "Carla!" I flinch as Walter screams at her from the other side of the paddock. "Move into your two-point faster and try a salad now and then!" *He's horrible.*

Carla pulls back on two straps of leather that restrain Milady's muzzle and slowly makes her way around. We lock eyes as she approaches, her mouth fixed in a hard line as her fiery eyes appraise me. *What's her problem?* Milady comes to a stop and Carla swings her leg across to dismount the animal. Her rider's garb is reminiscent of Walter's with the addition of a long-tailed overcoat. She unstraps her black helmet and cradles it at her side. "You look like crap, literally," she says, poking Mike in the chest.

I catch myself narrowing my eyes at her and forge a tight smile. Mike wafts his nose as he jokes back, "It would seem I'm not the only one stinking up the place."

"Please...no need to offend new members of your staff." She smirks at me, and I can't determine whether she means to insult me or not. "I don't believe we've met. I'm Carla," she says, extending a delicate, gloved hand.

I wipe my hand clean on my pants and slide into her grasp for a shake. "I'm Jane. You have a beautiful horse."

Carla lets out a sigh as she runs her hand through Milady's mane. "Beautiful doesn't get you into the winner's circle, unfortunately."

"I think the two of you put on a great show," I say.

"Thanks," she says, looking annoyed. She hands the leather straps to Mike. "Don't forget to groom her, please. Her tail is a little matted. Thanks, Mikey," she chirps and strides away from us.

When she is out of earshot, *Mikey* leans into me. "Sorry about that. She's actually nice when her dad's not around."

"Walter is her father?"

We exchange a look. "Yes, ma'am."

TWENTY-TWO

I AM ADJUSTING QUITE WELL to my new ranch routine. Although the work is laborious, my body grows strong, and my muscles have not been as sore. I can lift the bales of hay much easier. I toss my last bale on top of the neat pile I have assembled and place my hands on my hips, admiring my work. "That's about the cleanest stack of hay I've ever seen around here," Mike says, approaching me from behind.

"Oh, thanks," I say with a nervous smile.

He rubs his face gently. "Hey, I was wondering…Boots and Buster are overdue for a ride…would you be interested in riding with me? It's the perfect evening for it…"

"Really? You would take me with you?" I respond in disbelief. *He wants me? Me?*

A broad grin spreads across his face. "Sure, I would." As we approach the stalls, Mike tells me I'll be taking Buster, and he will ride Boots. I reach up to stroke Buster's long face, but he pulls away and lifts his head high above me.

I click my tongue to entice him, but he stamps his feet in protest. "No way I am doing this. He doesn't like me," I say, backing away from Buster's stall.

Mike shakes his head. "He just needs to figure you out. He's not sure whether you're a friend or foe." *Trust me, I know the feeling.* "Or…you could ride behind me?"

"We can do that?" I say, unable to hide the excitement in my voice.

"Of course. My dad used to take me tandem riding all the time when I was younger. We still have that same buddy saddle. It's made for kids so it's kind of small but honestly, I think you'll fit."

I fidget with anticipation. "Okay. I trust your expertise." As Mike saddles Boots, Carla struts over to interrupt our adventure.

"Isn't Jane a little too old to be riding your childhood tandem saddle, Mikey?" she asks, folding her arms across her chest. "And a Western saddle at that…you're such an American."

"Uh-huh. You're an American too, Carla. Riding an English saddle doesn't change your citizenship," he chuckles.

"Hmph. Try not to throw Jane off, okay?" With that, Carla turns on her heel and marches out of the stables.

Mike mounts Boots in one fluid motion. "You ready?" he calls down to me, extending his arm. I take his hand and slide my left boot into the stirrup. He pulls me up and behind him with ease. I instinctively wrap my arms around his waist and squeeze tightly. At this moment, I recall sitting behind Storm on a cloud, nervous for my first flight. A twinge of sadness overcomes me. *I hope Storm and Remedy are okay.*

Mike jerks his heel into Boots' side, and we are off. "Make sure to point your toes up in the stirrups and try to keep your back straight," he says, correcting my form. "And if you ride solo next time, remember to hold the reins with your thumbs up and wrists slightly in," he explains.

"Yes, sir," I say with a trace of sass.

Mike turns back, flashing me a mischievous smirk. "Hang on!" he orders, as he kicks his heels once more. I tighten my hold on him. *I never want to let go.* Boots breaks into a gallop, charging down the driveway I came in on what feels like ages ago. A warm breeze whips through my hair as we bounce along, sending fleeting waves of Mike's delicious scent into my lungs. My breath quickens with each jarring stride of Boots' powerful legs, thrusting me into Mike's body again and again.

Mike pulls on the reins and steers Boots down a tight trail. The terrain beyond the ranch is also breathtaking. The trees are different from the forest I know, but just as green and welcoming. After a short while, we trot across a flower-speckled meadow and Mike slows Boots to a halt. He dismounts and grasps my waist in his firm grip, helping me down. "We'll let Boots rest," he says, tying Boots to a tree.

We climb the slight slope of a hill overlooking the flowered clearing and take a seat side-by-side. "This is, by far, my favorite place to watch the sun set," he says.

"Oh? Do you usually bring Carla here?" I dare to ask.

He raises an eyebrow. "Carla? Never. The last person I brought out here was my sister," his voice cracks.

My heart aches for him as I watch the pain burn in his eyes. "What was her name?"

"Rachel…She would've liked you. And I can't stand the thought of her room layered in dust, reminding us that she's really gone. So, I'm grateful you're here." *Wow. He's deep.*

I nod respectfully. "Thank you for sharing her memory with me."

He stares into my eyes with a tenderness I've never known from a man. "You're easy to talk to."

"So are you," I say, nudging him gently with my shoulder. I watch the burning sphere retreat below the horizon. Its orange rays streak across a pink sky. "It's so beautiful."

"So are you," he says, gently nudging me with his shoulder. My eyes meet his and we stare at each other. His face is animated as we bask in the sinking sun. Panic courses through my veins as Mike courageously makes a small gesture—leaning into me until we are sharing the same breaths. Every fiber of my body has been aching for this moment but in the pit of my stomach, fear creeps in. *He doesn't know the truth about me, and I don't know if I could ever trust him with that. But I want to—desperately.*

Suddenly, I rise to my feet. "We should probably head back. It's getting dark," I say, flustered. Mike looks up at me, dumbfounded. His face falls as my words settle over him. He gives a slight nod.

"Of course," he says, rising to stand. We walk solemnly back to Boots. Mike retrieves a couple of carrots from a small pouch attached to the saddle and feeds one to him. "Here, this will help solidify your friendship," he says, handing me the other carrot. I take the carrot, grateful for his lasting kindness. Boots crunches it happily from my hand and snorts with pleasure.

Just as the last rays of sun give way to darkness, Mike unties Boots and climbs back into his saddle. After he helps me up, I latch onto his body tightly. I rest my head against his broad back as we journey back to the ranch, allowing the full weight of my regret to consume me.

TWENTY-THREE

ABOUT A WEEK AGO, I had my first trip to the "store" that everyone speaks of. Even though, as far as I've learned, there are many kinds of stores. And yet, if I were to say to another unsuspecting human: "I'm going to the store," they would know exactly what I mean. They would know that I mean the place where I buy fruits and vegetables and milk and all the things that freely surround me at no cost aside from the sweat of my brow.

Mabel took me on her last trip to the store for new clothes. The ones she and Chuck had loaned me when I first arrived had formerly belonged to Rachel and she was younger than I am. Not to mention, the sleeves have all decided to cut off my circulation in acknowledgment of my newly filled-out arms.

I also think they liked the idea of them not going to waste in a dusty closet better than the reality of them being torn and tattered by someone new. I don't blame them. I wouldn't want someone parading around in Mother's clothes, either. I don't even want to think about what has become of her things now.

I am reminded of our visit to the store as I collect the multicolored eggs in the henhouse. Mabel pointed out the vast selection of eggs during our outing—brown, beige, and white. No beautiful, speckled pastels to even speak of. None like the small bits of spring I cradle in my palms. I've since asked her why the eggs are all brown and white at the store and she said "Genetics". Whatever that means.

"Jane!" Mike calls loudly for me. I step outside to find him winded, with wooden sticks slung over his shoulder. "You'll never...believe...what I just...found." He's so breathless, he can barely get the words out.

"It's okay...just breathe," I say.

"I take it you've never played polo before?" He finally says once he has regained his composure.

"Never heard of it."

"Figures. I was cleaning out the barn and found these old mallets buried under a bunch of tools. It's been so long since I played, I thought it would be fun. Let's go find Billy and Carla!"

We hear Carla arguing with Walter before we see them when we enter the stables. "Your horse doesn't respect you. You must be stern!" Walter scolds as Carla slips off Milady's tack.

"She does respect me, Dad. But we've been working for two hours nonstop. She's just spent is all," Carla retorts.

"Oh? She needs a break, is that it? Hmph. By all means, take a few years off then. There's another Summer Olympics in, what, five years?" he seethes.

"What makes you think I will even qualify for next year?! There are so many competitors vying for those spots. The chances of me going all the way are slim to none and you know that. Just relax."

"Yeah, with that attitude you probably won't."

Mike clears his throat awkwardly. "Speaking of breaks...look what I found in the barn!" he exclaims, swinging the mallets down from his shoulder. "We can play polo! Jane and I against you and Carla. Whatta you say?" he asks Walter, offering his white smile.

Walter folds his arms over his chest. "That would hardly be enjoyable. Carla has been featured in the *North American Equestrian Magazine* three times, and—well—I trained her...We're professionals," he scoffs.

My eyes meet this man's determined scowl and no amount of convincing—even from someone as enticing as Mike—could talk me into playing anything with Walter. "I'll just keep score and leave all the playing to the *professionals*," I say. Mike looks at me to protest but I insist.

"You guys were gonna play without me?" Billy says, entering the stables wearing a look of disbelief. He sets aside the large bale of hay resting in his arms.

"No. You're welcome to play, of course," Mike replies.

"Alright then...two against two. Carla and I versus you and her pops," Billy suggests, winking at Carla.

I watch as Walter's eyes narrow in on Billy winking at his daughter. His nose scrunches, as if he has smelled something rotten. "Don't ever call me 'pops'," Walter hisses, pointing his riding crop at Billy, "And you will be on my team."

Billy's face falls but he obliges with a slight nod of his head. "Alright, that settles it. Billy and I will go make sure the pasture is clear of any animals and set up the goals. You two go ahead and make sure the horses are saddled and ready," Mike says.

While they set things up, I bring a stool from the barn to watch from the sidelines. I watch as the four of them enter the field on their horses. "Don't let me down, Mikey," Carla calls back to Mike, trotting behind her.

"I got you," Mike says, tipping his hat toward her. "First to four points wins," he adds, loud enough for everyone to hear. The two teams line up in the center of the field. Mike drops the ball beside him and strikes it with a steady swing. The ball arches up slightly and rolls down the field toward Billy and Walter's goal. Their horses take off after it. Billy is the first to get to the ball.

Swerving in front, he rears back to swing and misses the ball completely.

"ARGH! You idiot!" Walter yells in frustration, closing in on the ball himself.

"Hey, you're the one that wanted me on your team," Billy snaps. Walter huffs and launches up in his stirrups to stand. He slams the ball with one forceful swing, sending it speeding between Mike and Carla's goalposts. He trots in front of Mike with his mallet cocked over one shoulder. "One-nothing."

"Jane!" I suck in a sharp breath as Mike's smooth voice calls my name across the pasture. Our eyes meet. "Every time someone scores, you'll have to retrieve the ball and throw it back into the middle of the field." My cheeks flush as all eyes land on me, jogging out for the ball. With all my might, I hurl the ball back in between the two teams.

Mike is the first to take off toward the ball. Carla races down the field toward their goal. Mike connects with the ball, driving it forward in her direction. The field comes alive, sending tremors through my feet as the horses stampede across the grounds. Carla stops the ball expertly with her mallet and quickly pivots toward the goal. She maneuvers the mallet easily, her powerful swing sending the ball soaring with a crack. It arches a good four feet in the air before bouncing right through the center of their goalposts.

"Nice shot!" Mike screams excitedly, riding over to her. He grins from ear to ear as he holds his hand up high and Carla slaps it midair. I have seen the celebratory gesture a few times now but have never been on the receiving end. Probably because Carla gets them all.

As I run to get the ball, Walter chastises Billy until he is beet red in the face. I can't help but feel bad for the guy as he silently endures his rebuking. That is, until the cackle of Mike and Carla's obnoxious laughter echoes through the field. They continue to hammer the ball into the goal, bumping them into the lead.

I throw the ball in once more and Walter is all over it. Mike and Carla can't seem to stay on him long enough to make any contact with the ball. Billy is struggling but tries his best to stay in the vicinity of the action. Walter's thin frame commands his mallet with power as he whacks the ball farther and farther down the field. He has the ball all but sunk in the goal, just an instant away from scoring, when Mike zooms in to intercept it. With the mighty swing of his arm, the ball sails in the opposite direction, landing precisely inside the other goal. Mike relaxes in his saddle and rubs Boots gently on the neck. The horse lets out a tired sigh.

Walter sneers, "Three to one, your lead."

"I was right next to your goal when I made that last shot," Mike points out.

"So?"

"So, that was two points. That's game." Walter's lip curls up in an ugly snarl. He jams his heels into his horse's side and pulls up alongside Billy. Without hesitation, he thwacks the boy upside the head with the tip of his riding crop before speeding back into the stables.

"Ouch!" Billy cries, rubbing the back of his head.

Mike's smile is as wide as I've ever seen. His body glistens with a subtle sheen as he victoriously rides past me without a single glance, eyes glued to Carla. Her blond locks swish triumphantly down her back to the tune of her horse's high steps. How I yearn to go back to that private moment in the meadow, aching for Mike's lips to finally touch mine. But the thought provides little comfort, watching him so mesmerized by someone as talented as Carla. Someone as beautiful as Carla. Who am I kidding? Someone as human as Carla.

TWENTY-FOUR

BUSTER CRANES HIS THICK NECK to look back at me as I
sweep a brush over his glossy coat. His deep brown eyes
blink slowly. He lowers his head, letting me know he is relaxed in
my presence. We have come a long way from our first unfriendly
interaction. He trusts me now. It only took about a month and a
bushel of apples.

My free palm slides behind each stroke of the brush across
Buster's body until two sets of heavy footsteps trample into the
stables. Mike has his back to me as he takes Carla into his muscular
arms. She leans into him, joining him under the brim of his black
Stetson hat. He clasps her waist tightly and their mouths crash
against each other in a sudden fit of passion. *NO!!*

I instinctively duck lower into the stall and out of view. My
stomach turns as I peek at them again to witness what should be
my man all over that snooty girl. As they spin around entwined in
each other's arms, something most wonderful happens. The side
of Mike's face moves into a gleam of sunlight and that isn't Mike,
after all.

My mouth hangs agape as I watch Billy's hands invade Carla's hair, tugging her head backward to expose her neck. He kisses the nape of her neck all the way up to her right ear and suckles the delicate lobe.

"Get your hands off my daughter, you filthy swine!" All three of us jump as a furious Walter storms inside.

"Dad! Don't talk to him like that!"

"I'll talk to this no-account farm boy any way I well please!"

"Please, Dad! You're overreacting! Billy is kind and he cares about me."

"Sir, she's right. I do care a great deal for her," Billy utters. His cheeks redden as he nervously takes Carla's hand into his own as a sign of his goodwill.

Walter's eyes narrow in on the twining of their fingers, and he bites his bottom lip angrily. "You need to get out of my sight, if you know what's good for you, boy!" He slaps his riding crop across the palm of his free hand repeatedly. Billy turns his defeated face to Carla, who nods ever so slightly. He looks back to Walter one last time before bowing his head and dragging his feet outside.

"I cannot believe you would stoop so low! Have you no pride? Are you really so desperate that you would slum it with that greasy lowlife?" Walter asks his daughter.

"Stop it, Dad. I'm an adult and I'll make my own decisions concerning my love life."

"What about Mike?" I nearly fall over at the mention of his name. I unconsciously lean closer.

"What *about* him, Dad?"

"I've always thought the two of you would make for a fine match." My heart aches at the thought. Walter shakes his pointer finger, adding, "Besides, who do you think Chuck is leaving this ranch to? Just think of all the dollars we could squeeze out of this place." *So that's why he wants them to be together.*

"But Mike and I are friends. That's all we've ever been and all we will ever be." *Hope prevails!!*

"So, you're seriously going to date that loser? You would throw away all your hard work—your life?!"

"Billy has aspirations too, you know. You're just too self-involved to see beyond your own ambitions!"

"You better get your head out of the clouds, little missy, and focus on *your* ambitions before you wind up mucking out these stalls with that loser for the rest of your life!" Walter turns on his heel and rages back out of the stables.

I am silent as he unknowingly leaves me alone with Carla, her sobs streaking her makeup all over her already heartbreaking expression. Buster chews on his hay with little interest in Carla's sniveling until the sudden barking of the dogs spooks him. He neighs loudly and stamps his feet. I gently rub his backside and try to shush him but it's already too late. "Who's back there?" Carla snarls bitterly.

I hold my hands up with innocence as I step slowly out of the stall. "It's just me. I'm sorry—by the time you and Billy came in—"

"You saw us?" I nod my head uncomfortably, ashamed. "Isn't that just great? Not only have I been completely humiliated by my father in front of my boyfriend, but there was an entire audience I wasn't aware of."

"I don't know what to say…I feel terrible."

Her eyes refresh with tears anew and she collapses to her knees. "This is so typical of him, too. I knew he would never let me be happy with the man I love."

"Whoa. So, you love him then?"

She dabs her eyes with her hands and sighs. "Not that it matters…but yeah…I do."

"Of course it matters. Does Billy know how you feel about him?

"I don't know. We haven't said that yet."

I plop down on the floor beside her and drape my right arm around her shoulders. "I'm sure he feels the same way. Just look at you."

Her eyes lighten as I marvel at her still relatively intact beauty. "Why are you being so nice to me?"

I pause for a moment. "Let's just say, I know how it feels to have a father who is disappointed in you."

"Really?"

I nod. "More than you know."

She sniffles and rolls her shoulders back to sit up straight. "So, what about you? Are you ever going to tell Mike how you feel about him?"

My heart pumps a sudden influx of fresh blood into my cheeks. "Um. What do you mean?" I ask, gently sliding my arm back down to my side.

"Don't play dumb with me. It's obvious you're into him." *The gall of this girl!*

"Well, I…" My heart could burst at any moment from sheer embarrassment.

She smiles. "It's okay, I get it. But you should know he's nuts about you. Jabbers on and on about *Jane*. It's pretty annoying, actually."

"He does?"

She nods. "Want my advice? Kiss him. He's been dying for that ever since you two rode together a few weeks back." *He told you about that?* Carla hops to her feet and brushes herself off. "Dad will kill me if I don't get back to my training. Thank you—for talking with me and all."

I stand back up and hold my hands together in front of my hips awkwardly, nodding. "You're welcome."

"I mean it," she says and pulls me in for a hug. *Wow. This girl is full of surprises.*

I smile at her. "Anytime."

TWENTY-FIVE

IF I AM BEING HONEST, I have been anxiously awaiting this evening all week long. And it is finally here. *Yay!* The Anselmo family holds a small tradition known as "Family Movie Night" about once a month, but summer is an extremely busy time in the ranching business, and I have yet to be a part of such an exciting event. And sure, I still don't fully understand the appeal of watching other humans I have never met on a shiny, black screen (Mike tried earnestly to show me how to operate the television for a while), but the point is Mike will be there. I cannot help but swoon in anticipation.

Chuck sets up the projector outside while Mike arranges bales of hay around the screen. Mabel grabs some heavy quilts and extra throw pillows from inside and covers the bales dutifully. While the previews play, she runs back inside and returns with two large bowls of popcorn. Ace and Cooper follow closely at her heels. The dogs walk over to Mike, circle a few times, and curl up on either side of him.

Before long, we are all seated close, bundled up in a cozy paradise beneath the glow of a waning moon. *Stranger Than Fiction* is the film title and Mike tells us it's not his favorite Will Ferrell movie, but that it's still "pretty darn good". After watching all one hour and fifty-three minutes of it, I would have to agree. I have laughed, cried, and downright wept (the ending). I struggled with some minor areas of missing human context, but that's to be expected in my situation.

Chuck stretches his arms with a yawn. "I reckon it's about time I turn in for the night."

Mike's eyes flit from person to person. "So soon?"

The dogs get up slowly and dawdle toward the house. Chuck staggers to his feet. "Afraid so. Your old man is tired."

Mabel smiles at her son. "Your father and I are getting up there in years and we need our rest." *Up there in years. Ha. If she only knew how long my people live.* "But you kids go ahead and enjoy all that energy while you still can." She rises to her feet and places a soft kiss on Mike's forehead. "Goodnight, my son. Goodnight, Jane."

"Goodnight," Mike and I say in awkward unison as Chuck and Mabel head back inside. I deliberately avoid eye contact with him because he will know that I am not breathing. Well, maybe I am. Who can be sure at a time like this?

"Fifty first dates?" he asks.

My eyebrows jump automatically, and I meet his ocean eyes. "You said what?"

He holds up a DVD case. "*50 First Dates*...starring Drew Barrymore and Adam Sandler. Classic. Shall I put it on?"

"Oh, sure. Go ahead." I scoot down to the grass while he sets up the next movie, resting my back against a bale. He joins me on the ground and scoots in closer until his leg is rubbing against mine.

"I love this one," he says. I smile shyly and turn to face the screen. A chilly breeze nips at my neck, and I shiver. "Are you cold? Here." Mike pulls a quilt up over my shoulders and tucks it around my frame. "Is that better?"

My heart thumps uncontrollably under my shirt. "It is. Thank you." I am unbending as his body comes to rest against mine when the movie begins. His proximity has me too tense to assume any posture that isn't abundantly stiff.

"Just relax, Jane. It's me." The warmth in his voice is enough to subdue me. I exhale slowly and sink into his side, slowly melting until we are holding each other in an affectionate snuggle. And truthfully, I love this movie. I get to hear Mike's adorable laugh at the part where Lucy gives Ula a beating. I discover Mike's surprisingly squeaky voice when he sings about how nice it would be if we were older. And I see a glimpse. A glimpse of what love can look like. How one person can go above and beyond to accommodate someone else. Someone they care about.

My eyes are damp as the credits roll across the screen. "Did you like it?" he asks.

"Yes, I did. Good choice," I say, wiping my eyes with my sleeve.

He beams, pleased with my approval. "I had a feeling you would." We're quiet for a moment and then his eyes darken. There is a wild look there I don't recognize. *I'm terrified for Mike to learn the truth about me but he's so…irresistible. Carla better be right about this.*

I draw in a shaky breath and thrust my mouth onto his before I can change my mind. To my great delight, he embraces my boldness and presses his lips harder against mine. Our necks contort, from side to side, as the surface of his lips and tongue fervently explore mine for the very first time.

He inhales deeply when we finally pull apart, catching his breath as the electricity lingers between us. "That was a nice surprise," he says.

"I've been wanting to do that for a while," I admit, panting.

"Me too. I'm glad you finally did," he chuckles. He kisses my cheek and takes my hands into his. His eyes are serious as he tells me, "Jane, the more I get to know you, the more I want to know about you. I would like to take you on a proper date if you'll let me."

It takes me a moment to fully comprehend his words. My chest tightens as his request dawns on me. My voice quivers, "I would love that."

TWENTY-SIX

I KISSED MIKE," I TELL Carla the following day.

"You did?!"

I cover her mouth with my hand. "Shh! Keep your voice down!"

She peels my hand off and whispers, "I just can't believe it."

"It was your idea!"

"Yeah, but I didn't think you'd actually do it! So, how was it?"

"Um. It was," I let out a sigh, "amazing."

Carla gives a knowing smile. "I bet it was; the tension's only been building for months."

I look down sheepishly at my feet and then back up at Carla, unable to withhold my smirk. "And that's not all…he wants me to go out with him this Saturday."

"Oh my God! Are you serious—where to?"

"The 'R-Cade' I think he said?"

"Ooh, that's a good first date. You'll have so much fun. What will you wear?"

I have no idea what an R-cade even is so…no clue, but I obviously can't tell you that. "Um. I don't know yet. What would you wear?" I think to ask.

"Definitely shorts and a cute top," she says without hesitation. She surveys me with critical eyes. "You're welcome to borrow something," she quickly adds.

I blush. "Yes, please. I would greatly appreciate it."

"I'll bring some options for you to try tomorrow. You know, if things continue to go well, we could double date. You and Mike—and Billy and I."

"Yeah, that sounds like fun. How are you and Billy by the way? Everything okay after what happened with your dad?"

"Billy is understanding, thank God. But let's just say we won't be kissing at the ranch anytime soon."

Mike rolls a wheelbarrow inside the stables, and we are suddenly speechless. His eyes sparkle with humor. "Am I interrupting something?"

Carla and I exchange a look. "No. I was just leaving," she says, shooting me a secret wink. My anxiety soars as she leaves me alone with this human masterpiece.

He edges closer and strokes my cheek. "I missed you."

"I missed you, too," I say, beaming.

He leans down to let me sample a wet kiss. "I told my parents about us."

My heart stops. "You did what?!"

"Calm down," he laughs, "They're thrilled. They think you're wonderful." I gaze into his marine eyes and blush. "So do I," he adds with a sweet smile. I could flatter this man for days but refrain from fear of coming on too strong and losing this unbelievable opportunity.

"Do you need any help?" I ask, pointing to the wheelbarrow.

"As a matter of fact, I could use your help with something else."

"And what's that?" I ask.

A mischievous smile crosses his face. He motions for me to follow him as he retrieves Boots from his stall and walks him over to the wash stall. The black coat of the horse is dull in color, and his tail is too matted to swing with any sort of grace. Mike secures Boots and says, "Can you guess what time it is?"

I put my finger on my chin. "Let me think…" He chuckles and fills up a couple of buckets with warm water. I grab one of the buckets and squirt a few pumps of shampoo in. We stand shoulder-to-shoulder massaging Boots' muscular curves with soft, soapy sponges. I drench mine in the bucket and sling it across Boots' side. A sudden gush of water flies from my sponge, dousing Mike's white T-shirt. The front of his shirt clings to his skin, giving me a veiled glimpse of the definition that I've already come to memorize. "I'm sorry," I say, embarrassed.

I suspect he is angry when he continues to scrub the horse's body without a word, effectively ignoring my apology. I am ill at ease as I, too, go back to washing in silence. Several uncomfortable moments pass before I bend down to wash Boots' hind legs and a wet splash explodes across my back. Mike's laugh is infectious as he keels over, clutching his waist. I squeal with glee and launch my sponge at him, running to the other side of Boots for cover. Mike's eyes set with determination, and he bolts for me. We circle Boots a few times before Mike stops in his tracks, waiting for my next move. I stand there, motionless, while my heart pounds wildly inside of my chest.

Then he does the unexpected. The man dives headfirst under Boots and slides right to me. I scream and race out of the wash stall, laughing hysterically as I sprint across the stables. Mike's footsteps grow louder as he catches up to me from behind. A firm grip seizes my waist and jolts me to a stop in his arms. He whirls me around and gently shoves me backward until my back is on the wall.

He looks down at me with wanting eyes. "You're so beauti-ful," he says. His hands take turns running through my hair and I am swept away in the thrall of his kiss. We are both breathless when he reluctantly breaks away from me. *Whoa.*

"We better slow down," he says, more to himself than any-thing. His smile returns and he pulls me in for a tight embrace. "I'm so glad I met you," he whispers in my ear. *You have no idea.*

TWENTY-SEVEN

SATURDAY IS SLOW TO ARRIVE, but when it does, I am a bundle of nerves. I see Mike every day. He rests his head on a pillow, not twenty feet from mine, every night. But this is different.

I change into dark blue jean shorts and a simple white tee emblazoned with a tiny logo of a polo rider—both on loan from Carla. She had hoped I would wear her even skimpier, black crop top. I considered it all of four seconds before voicing a resounding no. I'm not entirely sure how human women attract human men, but I can't imagine it would begin by wearing something so open. Besides, Carla dates Billy. And not to side with Walter but...he's a bit of a dud.

Carla slathers my face with the goop she calls makeup. "Hold still," she snaps. I squirm under her touch as she grazes a soft brush over the edge of my cheekbone. The bristles tickle as they sweep over a sensitive patch of skin. After covering my blemishes, she blows out my hair and holds up a mirror. "What do you think?" she asks, smacking on a glob of pink bubblegum.

The woman in my reflection has a subtle golden-brown shimmer dusted on her eyes and a cherry-red kiss on her lips. Her eyelashes are longer and fuller. I run my fingers through the voluminous locks hanging seductively around her shoulders, mouth gaping. Carla crosses her arms. "Right? God, I'm good," she says, just as shocked as I am. *Goodbye, Plain Jane!*

She looks down at my chest and I blush. "That's interesting," she says, picking up the diamond from my necklace.

My mouth is suddenly dry. "Thank you. It was a gift from my mother."

She stares at me curiously. "You never talk about her," she says, and it isn't a question so much as a conclusion she's arrived at.

"Oh. Yeah, I guess I don't. She passed away last year. I miss her very much." My vision blurs behind budding tears.

"I'm sorry to hear that." She gently releases the stone to rest against my bosom once more. "Looks like you are all ready for your big date."

Before long, there's a knock on my bedroom door and Carla opens it to the man of my dreams. As per usual, Mike's classic white T-shirt hangs tantalizingly over his ribbed abdomen. *Look up! Look up!* His hair flows gloriously free about his face, while still managing to look kempt. And most importantly, his smile is genuine as he casts his stare on me. *I'm drooling, aren't I?*

"Where have you been all my life?" he asks in awe. The comment is sure to leave my face as red as the new lips I wear.

"You're not so bad yourself," I mumble nervously. He kisses my cheek and reaches for my hand.

"Uh-huh. Get a room you two," Carla quips.

"Hey, seriously. Thanks for making Jane look even more beautiful than she already does," he tells her, his eyes still trained on me. He assesses me from top to bottom and licks his lips almost imperceptibly before tearing his eyes away from me to face Carla. "We better get going!" he says excitedly.

His black truck is sleek and shiny as we approach and Mike, always the gentleman, stands behind my door after opening it for me. "After you." When I slide inside, the leather seat feels cool as it grazes the back of my thighs. The interior smell has a manufactured quality to it but still whiffs of freshly laundered cotton.

Mike enters the truck from the other side and cranks the engine. "You're going to love this place," he assures me. "It will take about a half hour or so to get there, though."

"I can't wait," I say, staring out the window at the clouds sinking into the mountains. He clears his throat, and I can't help but to check on him. His eyes are waiting for mine and then he looks down at his empty palm. His eyebrows are raised, as if to signify something amiss.

My heart races as I stretch my arm closer, but when my hand slides into his I have never felt anything more natural in my life. I relax into a sudden stillness, taking in the beautiful views whooshing past my window and the constant warmth in the man seated beside me. "Tell me something I don't know about you," he says after a while. *Oh, where to begin? What can someone as boring as me even confess? The only thing that comes to mind is the colossal secret I carry. The one I can never share with a human.*

"Hmmm. That's a good question...why don't you go first while I think about my answer?" I say.

He hesitates, thinking. "Okay, here's something. The name Michael is of Hebrew origin and means 'who is like God?' or 'gift from God'."

"Oh wow. That's pretty cool. I have no idea what Jane means."

"God is gracious," he says, automatically. "I looked it up." *He looked up my name?!*

A smile consumes my face. "When did you do that?"

His cheeks flush crimson. His voice is low and husky when he replies, "The night we took Boots for a ride and watched the sunset."

"I hated that night..." my voice trails off.

A tinge of hurt appears in his eyes. "You did?"

"I was sure I ruined our connection." My face is fixed on the floor, reliving the agonizing memory of snubbing his kiss.

He picks up my hand, still intertwined in his, and brings it to his supple lips. He presses a soft kiss into my skin. "I think that would be near impossible. I am completely smitten with you." A tingly sensation courses through my body, rendering me speechless.

He looks over to gauge my reaction. "It's okay, you don't have to say anything. I know you feel the same way." He turns his eyes back to the road with an air of confidence. *He knows me so well and can even read my body language. How unusual in a man!*

We are the only car in the front parking lot at dusk. "Is it open?" I wonder aloud.

"You bet. And it looks like we've got the whole place to ourselves." He hops out and opens my door before I can even unbuckle my seatbelt. "Come on, before it gets busy." He helps me down from his truck and we walk hand in hand. The moment we step inside, a frenzy of colored lights and loud sounds engage my senses.

I trail behind Mike as he walks to the counter, marveling at the vibrant colors glowing in the carpet underfoot. Hazy, purple lights gleam from the ceiling, enhancing all the hues of colors throughout the room. Mike is given a card by the large man behind the counter and told to come and find him if a game is out of order. "What do you want to try first?" Mike asks me.

I scan the room for the least intimidating piece of machinery I can find. My eyes pass over blinking equipment with flashy lights and urgent beeping sounds. A lump forms in my throat. *Why do I have to pick?* "How about that?" I point to a flat, white table undisturbed off in the corner.

He cracks a sly smile. "Air hockey? Are you sure that's a good idea?"

"Should we not?"

"We can," he says coolly, "it's just that no one has ever beaten me at air hockey before."

I set my shoulders back and fold my arms. "There's a first time for everything." *It can't be that hard. Right?* Mike chuckles and gestures for me to lead the way without a word. We stand on opposing sides, and he explains the basic rules of the game to me. He swipes the card, and the table comes alive with a soft, whirring noise. Mike slowly places the puck in front of his goal, and it slides a few inches to his left before he strikes it suddenly with his mallet. It shoots across the table and deposits directly into my goal before I can even flinch.

He leans forward onto the table and flashes his perfectly aligned teeth. *How did I ever get so lucky with this guy? He's enough to make anyone jealous of me...even Duplicity!* I imitate his movements as I launch the puck across the table. He sends it spinning around back to me, but I use my mallet to protect my goal and fend off his advances. I sink the puck in his goal a total of seven times back-to-back. *Yes! This game is awesome!* "Did you cheat?" he asks, scratching his head.

"How could I have cheated?" I ask, giggling. *Not too bad for my first time, eh, Mike? Never been beaten. Ha. Take that.* He shakes his head in disbelief and seems so legitimately shaken by the turn of events that I feel bad and refrain from performing a well-deserved victory dance.

As the night progresses, more and more people join us inside the arcade. But they may as well be invisible standing next to Mike. He and I play nearly every game, and it becomes very clear that my winning streak has ended. He beats me at racing games, fighting games, zombie games, even games of chance but I'm just happy to be occupying the same space as him. *He smells intoxicating…maybe even more so when he's sweaty.*

When we walk toward the door to leave, he pulls me through a curtain into a private booth. He inserts a five-dollar bill and the machine spouts off instructions. He wraps his arm around me, and I instinctively rest my head against his just as the timer counts down for our first picture.

I look at the clear lens of the camera and force a smile. *Click.* A bright flash blinds me momentarily and the countdown is already hounding us for a new pose. Mike sticks out his tongue and I do the same. *Click.* A second flash occurs and then Mike is staring at me again, his eyes dark and sultry. "I love you, Jane." Without any time to react, his mouth is locked on mine. *Click.*

TWENTY-EIGHT

I STARE ADORINGLY AT THE strip of black and white photos hanging from my vanity mirror. *He loves me!* There's a rapping on my door and I turn to see Mike standing in the open doorway. "Are you up for a drive?"

"Sure. Where are we going?" I ask, brushing my hair.

"There's somebody I want you to meet," he says pensively. He smiles and turns on his heel to let me finish primping. I twist my hair into a bun and follow him into the living room.

Chuck and Mabel break their stare from the baseball game on television to greet us. "Where are you kids off to?" Mabel asks.

"I'm taking Jane to visit Rachel." *Seriously? Visit her how? Can humans talk to the dead?* A pang of fear strikes me, and I swallow hard. But one glance at Mabel has me touched. Her eyes are bleary and shine with resilience.

"Bring her some fresh flowers, will you?" she says.

"I always do," he reminds her. Chuck nods respectfully and we scoot outside. Mike pulls out of the driveway slowly and drives in the direction of the trail we took Boots on for a sunset viewing. He slows to a stop near the meadow and shuts off the truck. "I always stop here to pick a few fresh flowers for her. I won't be long."

"I'd like to pick some with you," I say. Mike beams at me and comes around to pop my door open. The meadow is covered by pink and white flowers dancing in the breeze. We both collect a handful and hop back into the truck.

Soon, we are pulling up at a clearing dotted with ominous markers. Each block looms over wilting flowers. He is silent, leading me through the rows of gray stone. Most of the ground is carpeted with a hearty, green lawn. But unexplained feelings of loss and sorrow crush me when we pass the occasional rectangle of rich, brown soil.

When we come to stand before the slab of stone that reads "Rachel Anselmo", Mike places the flowers under it. A picture of a beautiful young girl is etched into the stone, bearing her brother's flawless smile. "She looks just like you," I tell him. "She's lovely."

He stares off, distracted. "We had a viewing after her death, and I almost didn't look. I didn't want that to be my final memory of her. But I just had to be sure it wasn't a mistake. I had to see it with my own eyes. And she looked so peaceful like she was dreaming, the same Rachel I remembered." It finally clicks that Rachel's dead body is buried where we stand, along with countless others. *How do human souls leave their bodies? Or do they? Does Mike not have a soul?* I shiver and loop my arm through his, seeking his comfort.

Mike looks down at his sister's face and then at mine. "At least her spirit lives on," he breathes. I hug him tightly and he melts into my arms. "Let's get out of here," he says.

On our way home, he surprises me by pulling into the parking lot of a charming ice cream shop. "I thought we were going home?" I say, confused.

"I wanted to swing by here first. Rachel loved this place." Inside, we browse the tubs of flavors behind the smudged glass. "What looks good to you?" he asks me.

"This one looks interesting." I point to a frozen mound of lime green with dark, brown specks.

"That was Rachel's favorite," he says, his voice bittersweet. He nods, as if there really were no other option, and turns to the girl in pigtails behind the counter. "We'll take two cones of Mint Chip, please." The girl hands us our heaping cones and I follow Mike to a small table by the window. I watch him, licking the sides before they have a chance to melt.

He catches me ogling and dabs his mouth with a napkin, self-conscious of my gaze. "Hurry up, before it melts," he says. I heed his warning and take a large, cold bite. My teeth are in immediate pain, and I wince. "Careful," he chuckles, "or you'll get a brain freeze." *First, you tell me to hurry and now to be careful. Which one is it?*

Once the initial shock has worn off, I realize how incredible the ice cream tastes. I have heard the praises of this elusive treat but never had the good fortune of trying it. Mabel refuses to keep any in the house on account of her "hips". I lick some more ice cream and gulp it down. "I thought of an answer to your question, by the way," I say.

"What question?"

"You wanted to know something new about me." He nods encouragingly as he continues to munch on his cone. "I already told you a little bit about my mother, but I never mentioned my father and that's because he abandoned me before I was born. My mother knew who he was, of course, and refused to tell me even though her death was imminent."

His mouth opens and the melted cream threatens to leak from his lips. He drags the back of his right hand across his mouth. "Wow, that's messed up. I'm so sorry."

"I was angry at first, but my mother was very strategic. She always had a purpose behind her choices, and she would never do anything to hurt me. So, I trusted her. I found out who he was right before I left home…and she was right to keep him from me."

"Is that why you left?" he asks, concern lining his face.

"Er—sort of. One of the reasons." I expect him to quiz me further, but he doesn't. The supportive look in his eyes lets me know that he's willing to listen to as much of my story as I am comfortable sharing, no more and no less.

"That must have been hard. But I'm eternally grateful you were pushed onto my path, no matter the reason," he says brightly. His compassion is liberating, and my lungs expand, as if a great weight has been lifted off my chest.

I savor this moment, falling more in love with him with every spoken word. "I love you, too," I boldly confess.

TWENTY-NINE

LOVE HAS BURNED IN OUR hearts for five months and seven days. Mike is all the things I have ever wanted in a partner, and I could not be happier. If only I had known this love was in my future when I was struggling back home. It would have given me some peace and strength to endure all my hardships.

I stand enchanted under the rustic Douglas fir Christmas tree in the living room. Multicolored lights twinkle within the branches and burlap bows dress the tree. Decorative ornaments hang without a fuss, ranging from old to new. Presents are piled high under the tree, encircled by a small locomotive on a railway leading nowhere. Even the fallen needles sprinkled over the gifts add to the spirit of the holiday.

The cool weather and cheer in the air remind me of last year's Winter Solstice, something I have come to learn that humans do not celebrate. Instead of a single great feast, they stretch their holiday across the entire month of December—even bleeding into some of November and January. That's probably why so many of them are, well, on the heavy side.

Mabel and Chuck have already gone to bed, and Mike and I sit on the floor by the crackling fire wrapping their gifts with the dogs curled up nearby. I fold the blue wrapping paper, embellished with sparkly white snowflakes, neatly around the box of the cashmere sweater I purchased for Mabel. "You know, Mom's had that sweater in her online shopping cart for months. She's going to be ecstatic tomorrow when she opens it," he says.

"Really?" I ask.

"She'd feel too guilty to spend that kind of money on herself. Even though she deserves about a hundred sweaters as far as I'm concerned." I tape up the last corner of the package and press a snowman sticker gift tag on top. In my neatest penmanship, I scrawl Mabel Anselmo on the 'To' line and Jane underneath, next to 'From'.

Mike stares at the package for a moment, scrutinizing my manuscript. "What?" I ask, defensively.

"Nothing," he chuckles. "It's just that I'm now realizing I don't even know your last name." I don't look up to meet his eyes and instead grab for the next present to wrap, pretending I didn't hear him. "Jane?" he presses.

I reluctantly face him and let out an annoyed sigh. "Does it matter?"

One corner of his mouth turns upward into a subtle smirk. "Well, excuse me, but I think I should know my girlfriend's last name," he says, amused. I shoot him a look that I don't often use as a warning. He raises an eyebrow, sensing his mistake but unable to locate its source. "What? Is your dad the ringleader of some kind of crime syndicate?"

"I know you think you're being funny but you're not. And I don't want to talk about it." I stand up, dropping the half-wrapped gift from my hands, and storm outside, letting the screen door slam behind me. An opportune rush of cold air hits my face and it's the only thing preventing me from having a panic attack. I try to slow my breathing as I watch the snow fall silently around the porch.

The screen door creaks behind me, and I don't have to look to know it's Mike. He would never let me walk away that easily. He gently pulls my chin toward him with his index finger, and I see his worried face, all trace of humor gone. "What's really going on here? Why are you so upset over something so small?" His question is reasonable, and I wish it were simple enough to merit an answer.

I clench my eyes to stop the tears from pouring down my face, but they don't. I jerk my chin from his grip and walk toward the other side of the porch, ashamed. My voice comes out in a hoarse sob, "I don't have one."

"How is that possible?"

"You would never understand," I blubber, unable to maintain my composure any longer.

"Try me," he says with calm authority.

"I want to tell you more—I truly do—but it would change everything between us and jeopardize not only my safety but countless others as well."

Concern creases his brow. "Baby, what's wrong?" Mike comes over to me and ushers me to the porch swing. He sits me down, taking both of my hands in his. "Jane, I would never do anything to hurt you in any way. I want you to trust me and know that anything you tell me stays between us."

I pull one of my hands away reflexively to rub my furrowed brow. "I don't know, Mike. I'm scared. If I tell you, you will never look at me the same again."

He wipes the fresh tears from my cheeks, his warm thumbs soothing me. "I promise you; I will always do everything in my power to protect you. I swear it on Rachel's grave." At this moment, I believe in my heart that what he tells me is true. I can always confide in him.

I take a deep breath and begin to tell him my story from the beginning. An incredulous look takes permanent residence on his face as I confess the details of my former life. It's clear he is skeptical of my past and where I come from but listens to me for hours on end, asking any number of questions. I answer them all truthfully. "...And since my powers never came in, I can't even prove any of this to you. You'll just have to take me at my word."

I hold my breath, waiting anxiously until he finally speaks. "Jane, sweetie, I want to believe you but listen to what you're saying. I'm sorry—but that's just crazy talk. Now, listen to me. I love you. But you need to see someone about all this, and I'm not saying that to hurt your feelings. I'm no expert, but that sounds a lot like repressed feelings and trauma to me. I've seen the TV shows."

"Wait! I can prove it!" I say excitedly.

His eyes flash with anger. "Jane, just stop with the lies. I'm starting to get upset."

"Trust me. Wait right here." I dash inside and dig through the bottom of my sock drawer until I find that which I seek. I return to him out of breath. "Okay, now hold out your hands, palm-side up." I can tell that he's getting annoyed, but he indulges me. "Take a good look," I say. We stare down at his hands, studying the deep lines and calluses. The hardened crests bordering his fingers and palms remind me of a mountain range.

"This better be good," he says.

"I was saving this. Just so you know," I mutter. I place the opal gemstone Remedy had given me into his right hand. "Now rub the sides of it between your fingers and then hold your hands tightly around it."

He does as I say and the stone glows in his hands. When he opens them again, his palms are moist and soft, the swirls of his identity the only marks that remain.

Mike is stunned, dropping the stone back into my hand with a shiver. He stares at his unblemished hands before running one through his hair in disbelief. I can tell by his expression that he's starting to piece it together—all the little jokes that went over my head and my relative ignorance of all things human.

"Let me try and just wrap my brain around this for a moment," he says. He is silent while he thinks, studying me with inscrutable eyes. The rapid thumping of my heart is the only sound I hear as I patiently wait for him to come to terms with what I am. "So, you're telling me…you're a…" he stifles a laugh before continuing, "…a fairy?"

"How dare you say that to me?" I snap, taking a step away from him. He gains back the distance lost by stepping toward me.

"Did I say something wrong?" he asks.

I must fight the urge to roll my eyes. "There is no greater insult among my kind."

"Okay, now I'm really confused. I thought that's what you've been trying to tell me."

"My people are called the Fairkind," I say, setting the record straight.

He chuckles. "Sounds weird."

"Weirder than saying," I lower my voice to the softest whisper I can manage, "*fairies?*"

His eyes brighten. "Maybe."

"And your thoughts on the term mankind?"

"Okay. I guess it's not that weird," he admits.

"How do you even know about—" A light comes on from inside the house causing me to pause. I peer through the window, watching Mabel's head disappear into the fridge, no doubt on a quest for a midnight snack. I turn back to Mike and continue my question, "—*fairies?*"

"Everybody knows about them—I mean—most people don't actually believe they're real."

I fold my arms across my chest. "Here I am, *really* in the flesh."

"Yeah, well, you're supposed to be the size of my thumb with little wings."

"That's ridiculous. Who would believe that?"

"You'd be surprised." Mike holds his thumb up next to my face and squints his eyes. "Yep. Bigger than a thumb. And the politically correct term is Fairkind. Noted." He bops me on the nose with a smile. *I could never stay mad at you.* "Your secret is safe with me." He pulls me in for a tight embrace and strokes my hair. "Thank you for telling me," he breathes in my ear, holding me close.

Over his shoulder, I peek up to see that the moon has a very distinct red sheen to it as it does from time to time. "Oh wow," I say, surprised. "Look."

Mike follows my gaze upward. "That's right. I completely forgot about the blood moon."

"It's beautiful," I say, mystified. But when I turn back to face Mike, his eyes are affixed to me.

A look of urgency floods his face, and he stammers, "J-Jane, I have loved you since that first time I laid eyes on you, stepping out of my dad's truck. I knew right away that you were the girl for me. And as I've gotten to know you, that has only been confirmed time and time again. I never want to be without you. I was hoping I could last until tomorrow before I posed you this question, but I don't think I can wait anymore."

Before I can even speak, Mike kneels on one knee before me, another gesture I'm not familiar with. He reaches into his pocket and presents me with a small box. He opens it toward me, and I gasp. A skillfully cut diamond twinkles against the black velvet that cushions it. He clears his throat. "Jane—of the Fairkind—will you marry me?"

An instantaneous smile spreads across my face. I throw my arms around his neck, knocking us both to the ground. As I lay on top of him, staring into his extraordinary face, I finally give him my reply. "Yes!"

THIRTY

THE PAST SIX MONTHS HAVE been a whirlwind of planning our wedding while balancing work on the ranch. The hardest part of which proved to be obtaining legal documents for myself. Fortunately for us, Billy runs with a bit of a riffraff crowd, so he was able to secure some surprisingly impressive counterfeits. Mike told him my dilemma and desire to remain hidden from my depraved father, excluding the details of my ancestry, of course. Billy was remarkably sympathetic and asked no questions.

I haven't seen Mike all morning and I won't until I walk down the aisle to become his wife this evening, the anniversary of our very first date at the arcade. Carla steps away from my face with her brush and eyeshadow palette in hand and gasps, "You look stunning." Mabel nods her head, sobbing. She hasn't had a dry eye all morning.

She snaps a quick candid of Carla and me admiring my glamorous reflection. "Alright, darling," Mabel sniffs, "Let's get you into this gown."

I eye the flowy dress hanging on the rack and my heart skips a beat. I reach for my diamond necklace and roll it between my fingers. *Thank you, Mother, for leading me to Mike.* I slip out of my silky robe and take Mabel's outstretched hand as she and Carla help me step into my gown. Mabel fastens the last button on my dress and she's crying again. "Stop or you're going to make me cry!" I say.

"I just spent hours perfecting your makeup, so you better not," Carla snaps.

I hand Mabel a tissue and she dries her eyes. "I'm sorry. I'm just so happy Chuck found you all that time ago. You have touched our lives, Jane. You are such a blessing to this family."

"Okay, now I'm going to cry. Cut it out you two," Carla says. I smile and squeeze Mabel's hand, pulling her toward me. Carla comes to stand on the other side of me and all three of us gather around the floor-length mirror, taking in the dress fit for a princess. A delicate sleeve of floral lace hangs elegantly off each of my shoulders. The bodice cinches at my waist and then cascades into a sheer, white curtain of tulle that brushes the ground ever so slightly.

I find myself swaying as Carla and Mabel flatter me with compliments of my outstanding grace and beauty. Carla snaps one last selfie before it is time for me to finally receive a real last name. Billy and Chuck are waiting to escort Mabel and Carla when we step out of the house. "My, oh my. What a sight to behold you are, dear," Chuck says lovingly to me.

"Yeah, I guess under all that horse dung, you look alright," Billy teases. Carla delivers a playful slap on his arm. "You, *however*, look smokin' hot, babe," he tells her, twirling her once for a full view.

We giggle and then I am serious when I say, "Thank you all for your kind words. And for supporting me and Mike. It means a lot." My breath quickens with every step we take toward the barn where I am to be wed. We stop just outside of the entrance to wait.

Mabel straightens Chuck's boutonniere and smoothes her hair one last time. Chuck lifts her lined hand to his mouth and kisses it softly. "Are you ready for another daughter?"

Her eyes well up yet again. "Absolutely," she says hooking her arm through Chuck's. The wail of a violin hums through the barn beckoning our entrance. Chuck and Mabel disappear inside first, followed too quickly by Carla and Billy. The cheerful melody slows to a tender ballad, and it is my turn. I grab my necklace one last time before stepping into the rest of my life.

Standing front and center, my handsome man is waiting for me in a perfectly tailored black tuxedo. The moment he sees me, he raises his hand to his mouth to choke back the tears. I sweep my eyes over his extended family, all turned to face me, but a brooding Walter steals my stare for longer than I would've liked. I shake my head gently and return my eyes to Mike, my home. I float down the aisle until he is taking me by the hand under an archway of fragrant, white flowers.

"You're breathtaking," he leans to whisper in my ear as we join hands. I keep my stare steadfast on this handsome man and his smile. We say our vows and exchange rings and then we are knitted together for no man—or Fairkind—to separate. His excitement is palpable as he dips me back and dives into my kiss.

Every hand in the audience applauds us as we turn to face them. Our cake is decadent, and the gifts are generous, but I am pining for the moment I can finally have my husband all to myself.

We practically peel out from the ranch once we have satisfied the minimum time requirement expected at this type of social gathering. Mike ropes his arm around me and pulls me across the front seat until I am seated in the middle, by his side, for the long drive to our honeymoon suite. Our destination: Seattle. We grab fast food for a snack on the road, finally arriving at the hotel a little after ten o'clock p.m. We are both exhausted from the car ride, but the warm lights pouring outside from the lobby of the five-star hotel reinvigorate us.

Mike leaves his truck with the valet, and they tell us they will bring our luggage up to our room momentarily. We walk arm in arm toward a front desk agent bearing the most pleasant smile I have ever seen from someone inside the confines of their employment. "Checking in?" she asks in a voice just as affable.

"Yes, ma'am. The name is Anselmo," Mike says.

"Yes, sir. And I see here in my notes that you have chosen to celebrate your honeymoon with us. Congratulations!" she says politely.

"Thank you," Mike says, kissing me fondly on the forehead.

"Here are your keys. I've written down your room number and the Wi-Fi password for you. The elevator is just down the hall," she says, gesturing with a very professional open palm. "We sincerely hope you enjoy your stay, Mr. and Mrs. Anselmo." *Whoa. Mrs. Anselmo? I could get used to that.*

Mike collects our keys and escorts me to the elevator, his eyes never leaving me. When we locate our room, he picks me up and carries me inside. He gently lays me down and I sink into the first bed we will ever share. I am so enamored with the man I love that I fail to see the bouquet of red roses adorning the coffee table or the tray of chocolate-covered strawberries waiting for us on the intimate candlelit table outside on the balcony. It isn't until a breeze blows through my hair that I notice these things and the open doors inviting us to a romantic evening under the stars.

Mike spots his suitcase on the luggage rack and unzips it, producing a slim bottle of champagne he had stashed away for our first night as husband and wife. He pops the cork, fills two flutes, and passes one of the glasses to me. "Cheers," I say, accepting the glass.

"Cheers to you, Mrs. Anselmo." He clinks his glass with mine and gulps the fizzy wine back in one swallow. *At least I'm not the only one who's nervous.* He leads me outside and pulls my chair out for me in true gentlemen's fashion. He proceeds to hand-feed me chocolate-covered strawberries for the better half of an hour.

Soon, our bellies are as content as our hearts, and we look toward the sparkling cosmos above us. We sip our champagne and stargaze until one bursts across the sky, falling before our eyes.

"Look," Mike says, pointing. "A shooting star."

I smile sweetly at him. "We call it skyfire."

"I like that better. Why do you guys get all the cool stuff?"

He makes me giggle before I can go on, "If you see skyfire in my culture, it is a sign of new beginnings for you. A new life even."

"That seems fitting. We, humble humans, make a wish whenever we see one."

I grin. "And what will you wish for?"

His eyes darken for the first time today. "I wish you would come closer to me." His eyes stay locked on me as he takes me by the hand and guides me to the edge of the bed. *I can't believe this is about to happen.* He advances toward me and takes me into his arms. His kiss is sensual, and we make love for the very first time. Things are a little bumpy at first, but we laugh off the awkwardness without fear. *We have plenty of time to get this right.*

We spend a few days in Seattle, seeing all the sights it has to offer. We wander through local markets and share a kiss above the bustling city at the top of the Space Needle. But it takes no time at all for me to grow homesick. Five-star dinners are fine and well but my stomach yearns for the simplicity that comes from Mabel's home cooking. My terrific husband, Mike, who is skillfully attuned to my wants and needs, identifies how I am feeling straight away and convinces me to spend the rest of our honeymoon in the privacy of our room, getting to *know* each other again and again.

When our reservation comes to an end, we pack up our things and head back to the ranch. As we pull up, we stare bewildered at a commotion of strangers shuffling in and out of the barn. Mike parks the truck and we step outside, unloading our luggage. "Surprise!" Chuck and Mabel shout in unison.

"What's happening?" Mike asks. We approach them slowly, unsure of what exactly it is we are being surprised with.

"We didn't want you and Jane to have to squeeze into the same bedroom you've had since you were in diapers, so we hired a crew to convert the old barn into a separate apartment for you. But don't look yet! It isn't finished. A bigger barn is being constructed on the other side of the property for the animals."

"Oh, my goodness. Thank you all so much," I say, overwhelmed with gratitude for the humans I have grown to love more than my own kind.

Mike drops the suitcases to hug his father tightly. Chuck claps his son proudly on the back. "We love you both and wish you every happiness together." *What a great father.*

THIRTY-ONE

BABY, WAKE UP." MY LEFT eye eases open to see my darling, Mike, leaning over me, dressed for work. "You overslept."

"Why didn't you wake me up sooner?" I ask, suddenly alert.

He shrugs. "You looked tired."

I spring from the bed and slide into some jeans. The sun is already beaming in through Mike's bedroom window. I yank a shirt over my head and fasten my belt.

He hands me a blueberry muffin saying, "Mom already put breakfast away. But I'll go warm something up for you if you'd like?" *Aww. I hope the honeymoon stage lasts awhile.*

"No, this will do. Thanks, babe," I say and take a bite of the muffin. He tries to squeeze around me to head for the door, but the queen-size bed stops him. We both turn sideways and slide out of each other's way. There's a loud thud and then he's coiled over, shrieking in agony.

"Ow!" he yelps, hopping on his right leg, and clutching his left foot with his hands.

"What happened to you?" I ask.

"I stubbed my toe," he snarls, his angry eyes shooting daggers at his unsympathetic bed. "Not much longer until the barn is finished. I can't wait," he mumbles, trying to suppress his aggravation as he stands up straight. "You wouldn't happen to have any more of those magic stones, would you?" he asks, his tone already improving.

I frown. "I'm fresh out." I move toward him and rub his back softly. "Are you gonna be okay?"

He lets out a long sigh. "I'm fine." Mike leaves his room and heads outside. I rush to finish my muffin, brush my teeth, and step into my boots to bolt for the stables. And that's where things get weird.

"Good morning, Walter. Carla," Mike says, tipping his hat. His chipper greeting leaves me in awe of the man I have the privilege of calling mine. He has plenty of opportunities to let things dampen his good nature, but he never does. He is the most optimistic person I know, despite his share of hardships.

"Right back at ya," Carla says. Walter nods without any other movement and turns his gaze back to Carla, tacking up Milady.

"Wouldn't kill you to be nice every now and then, jerk," I hear Mike bark.

I snap my head to gape at him, astonished by his ill-mannered remark. "Mike! That was rude," I scold him. Walter isn't my favorite person either, but the Mike I know would never speak to someone like that.

"What was?" Mike asks, confused.

"What you just said to Walter, obviously," I say, leaning into my heel.

"Good morning?" he repeats.

"Quit playing dumb. We all heard it," I snap.

"I don't think we did…" Carla says, leading Milady closer by the reins. "What did he say?" she adds. Walter's face is as bewildered as Mike's as he stares at me, waiting for my answer.

"Maybe I should've let you sleep longer," Mike says.

I face him once more. "Don't even start with me."

"Honey," he laughs uncomfortably, "I haven't said anything."

I look at their three faces, each puzzled. Walter's mouth twitches and I hear him say, "He married this nutcase over my award-winning daughter," even though his mouth never opens to talk. *What is going on?*

"Excuse me. I think I'm unwell," I say, quickly turning on my heel and running for the house. Mike follows closely behind, shouting for me to stop. But I won't until I'm in the living room, plopping on the couch to bury my face in a pillow.

He takes a seat next to me and reaches for my hands. I slowly meet his eyes. "Care to explain?" he says.

"I don't know exactly. But I have a theory."

"I'm all ears."

"First, tell me this, did you call Walter a jerk?"

"Not...out loud."

I lean forward unconsciously. "But you thought it?"

Mike nods, looking guilty. "How'd you know?"

"I'm guessing my powers finally decided to come in."

"Interesting...So, then what am I thinking right now?"

I stare at him, unamused. "I don't know. I can't control it or anything."

"Sure, you can. Come on, just try. We'll start with something easy." He jiggles with excitement as he twists my body around until we're sitting face-to-face. "Now, what number am I thinking of?"

I roll my eyes. "This is stupid."

"Yeah, but it'll be fun." I exhale slowly and focus on his eyes like Fairmaster Beguile had taught us. I hear nothing except the squeaking fan above us spinning for two full minutes.

"I give up."

"Baby, keep trying. I know you can do it." He says it so confidently that I start to believe I might be able to. I stare at him intently, pursuing his thoughts. They're almost within reach…I gasp dramatically.

"Fourteen," I announce.

"That's it! Fourteen! How about now?"

"One hundred and ninety-two."

"And now?"

I stare at him cautiously, unsure of myself. "Are you trying to trick me?" I ask. He shakes his head. "Pie?"

"Yep. 3.14," he says.

"Huh?"

"Never mind that—you got your powers!"

"I guess so. Weird."

"So cool." He leans back against the couch, resting his head on the cushion with a smile. "My wife is a superhero…Should we go get some lotto tickets?" He winks.

"I'm trying to blend in here, remember? And I have a feeling that me winning the Powerball is going to make that difficult. Besides, tempting doesn't work like that." I rub my temples. "Ugh. This is not good."

"Don't stress about it." He squeezes my hand. "Just because you have powers doesn't mean you have to use them."

"I guess you're right." *But why now, after all this time?*

"I better get back to the stables," he says reluctantly. "There is a lot of work to do today. But take your time. No rush." He kisses me on the cheek before he walks out the door. I sink back into the couch. The arrival of my Offering scares me, threatening to snatch my new life with Mike away if I am discovered. And yet, I can't stop smiling. *I guess I'm not so broken, after all.*

THIRTY-TWO

I WAKE UP TO A splitting headache. Mike hands me a couple of pain relievers, or human healing stones as I like to call them. I gulp them down with a big swallow of orange juice and wait for the pain to subside. Soon, the throbbing dulls until I forget all about it.

I get straight to work in the garden, fertilizing the crops and pouring my watering can over the sprouting greens. I lift the insect nets to check the development of our runner beans, squash, tomatoes, and peppers, which are all coming along nicely. But before too long, I grow weary and need to sit down for a bit. *Why am I so tired all of a sudden?*

My mind muses on all the recent changes to my life while I rest. Thankfully, it only took a few days to get my Offering under control. I am no longer bombarded with the obtrusive thoughts of others. And I am proud to say I can access people's thoughts when, and only when, I choose to. Which is never. Invading someone's private thoughts seems like a downright lousy thing to do, much less commanding someone to do my bidding.

I exhale loudly and lug myself to my feet. I don't know where it comes from, but my eyes are suddenly tear-stricken. Streams run down my face, overwhelming me with emotion I can't even identify. And things get weird again.

The bluest of skies is quickly overtaken by a wave of dark clouds rolling across the length of the garden. I look up, apprehensive of the spontaneous weather, just as the first drop of rain splats against my forehead. A few peals of thunder crack and I run toward the house, only to discover the air just outside the garden is warm and dry from a scorching sun. *That's odd.*

My emotions are stifled by the strange anomaly. And in the blink of an eye, the clouds are gone, and all is right in the world again. *Did I do that? What is going on?*

I shake my head, dazed by the strange sight. I look around to see if anyone else has witnessed it, but I am alone. I sigh. *Let's try this again.* I stand up tall and march back into the garden.

Reaching into the bed of newly damp soil, I tug on some stubborn weeds trying to smother the roots of our fall carrots. When I manage to yank one out, the nearby little fronds explode through the soil, until they are hanging off the largest carrots I've ever seen. *Oof. That's not good.*

I gently place my hands on one of the log-sized carrots as my heart pounds in my chest. *No. No. No. Please, go back to sprouts!* The carrots implode on themselves and snap back into the soil in an unbelievable sight. My jaw hangs agape as I stare down at my unexceptional hands. *I've been gone so long that I forgot what magic looks like.*

*Tempting, conditioning, growing…so that means…*I gasp loudly. *I have all the Offerings?* I graze my fingers over my chapped lips to test my theory, and they instantly plump with moisture. *Healing. Pretty handy, I gotta say. But how am I going to hide all of this?*

Well, I brush my hands together and do what any nonhuman would do in my very-much-human-shoes. I ignore the revelation of my new powers and get back to work.

THIRTY-THREE

MIKE AND I HAVE BEEN thoroughly enjoying our new residence, the old barn, even falling victim to the most humanistic thing of all—consumerism. What I mean by that is my new overindulgence in decorations and knickknacks, which are of no actual use and therefore nonexistent where I come from. *But they're so pretty.*

Every moment not spent in our daily toils on the ranch we find ourselves basking in our cozy new home, specifically the bedroom quarters. But as the rooster crows, signaling another new day, we must pry ourselves from between our silky sheets.

My day begins as any other: turning out the horses, mucking out the stalls, collecting eggs from the henhouse, milking the cows, tending to the garden, and feeding the animals. But my prospects for the evening change dramatically when Carla approaches me with an invitation. "Have you heard?" she exclaims. "The fair is in town! Billy and I are going tonight at seven. Would you and Mike want to join us?"

Having never heard of such a thing, I hesitate before giving her an answer. "Let me see if Mike has anything planned and I'll get back to you if that's alright."

"Okay. I hope you guys can come. It'll be so much fun." Carla tucks her hair back into her helmet and hops on Milady for a few more laps around the course.

I don't bump into Mike until the clock strikes five and we both head inside the main house for dinner. He gives me a tender kiss on the cheek even though a visible layer of filth coats my skin. "How was your day, babe?" he asks me.

"Buster had a shoe come off, so I had to deal with that. I called the farrier to see when he was available to come out and reattach it, but he won't be able to swing by until next week."

"Did you wrap his hoof in the meantime?"

"What do you take me for—some kind of amateur?" The newfound confidence in my tone surprises me just as much as him by the face he wears. What a change from a year ago. "Oh, and Carla invited us to the fair tonight…I wasn't sure if that was something we would be interested in…?" I say, eyeing Chuck reading his paper at the end of the table. It's a relief that Mike knows the questions I'm really asking him which are: 'What is the fair?' and 'Would I like it?'

His eyes light up immediately. "Oh, yeah. We're interested," he says, looking at me with a childlike grin. Over dinner, Mike asks Chuck and Mabel to join us for the night out, but they decline. After we have showered and changed, they wave us off and we climb into Mike's truck.

"So, are you going to tell me anything about this fair before we get there?"

"And ruin the surprise? I don't think I will," he says with a smirk.

I fold my arms across my chest in playful protest. "Well, I better like it."

"Trust me, you will." We turn down a dark dirt road, and I see a cluster of colorful lights beaming in the distance. A giant wheel of baskets turns about slowly amidst the delighted screams of its passengers.

I look at Mike in disbelief. "Is that where we're going?"

"Yes, ma'am." His grin is reminiscent of those found in his childhood photos displayed proudly on Mabel's fridge. He opens my door, and I cling to his side as we approach the entrance.

It is easy to find Billy and Carla in the sea of people as they are the only two making out awkwardly in a corner. When they come up for air, Carla's eyes enlarge, having spotted us. She backs away from Billy and waves frantically. "We were wondering if you two were going to show up!" she says excitedly.

"It doesn't look like you were," Mike chuckles.

Carla rolls her eyes and adjusts the neck of her blouse which fell off her shoulders during their debauchery. "Nobody asked you," she snaps. Billy sniggers and taps his fist against Mike's.

"I guess we better go get in line," Mike says, wrapping his arm around me.

"Nah, that line is insane. I got a big booklet of tickets so we can all share," Billy says.

My senses are flooded at once with new sights and sounds as we enter the fairgrounds. Rides of all shapes and sizes twirl their passengers about in a chaotic frenzy. Lights flash in tune with the booming beats of hip-hop music. Sweet and savory scents from the food vendors intoxicate the crisp, evening air. "This is incredible. What should we do first?" I ask in wonder.

Carla points at four tall, wavy slides. "Ooh, let's start with a little slide racing," she says. We each grab a soft mat and climb the steep staircase to the top. "Whoever wins can choose the next ride," she adds.

"Say less," Billy says, using his long arms to launch himself down the slide. My heart flutters as I wait for the cue of the scowling ride attendant, irritated from Billy's unauthorized takeoff. Billy is already at the bottom when the man gives us the signal to start. Laughing uncontrollably the entire way down, I feel the thrill of each drop in the pit of my stomach. I flop onto the inflatable bed of air at the bottom seconds before Carla and Mike slide in behind me.

Billy stands over us with a disapproving look. "Took you all long enough. I pick the spaceship ride next. Hope you guys haven't eaten recently." He puffs his cheeks out, pretending to barf in his mouth while clenching his stomach.

"No, you cheated. It's Jane's pick," Carla says.

"Alright. Fine," Billy huffs.

I look around anxiously at the daunting death traps that surround us. "Hmm…how about…that one?" I ask, pointing to the high-flying swings.

"Are you sure you don't want to go on something closer to the ground?" Billy asks, fiddling with his hands uncomfortably.

I smile at Mike knowingly. "Heights don't bother me."

"This is why I should have picked," Billy grumbles.

"Is little Billy-boy scared?" Mike asks in his best baby voice.

Billy straightens, puffing his chest. "Nah, man. I ain't scared. I mean, I'll do it."

"Come on, babe. Let's take our relationship to new heights," Carla says, stroking his back. We strap into four adjacent swings and lift off. My stomach tightens as we rise higher and higher, feet dangling. I let the music consume me as the breeze whooshes through my hair with each revolution.

Mike reaches out for me as we soar through the air. I grab ahold of him, interlocking my fingers in his. When the ride is over, I beam under disheveled hair. "I love it!"

"I can see that," Mike chuckles from his neighboring seat. "How about you Billy, you good?" Billy nods but his face is pale.

The moment we are instructed to remove our safety harnesses, he is already bolting away from the platform.

"Now let's see how good your aim is," Mike says, leading us toward a large glass tank of water. As we draw nearer, I notice a man inside, hovering precariously. His face is painted stark white with a red nose and blue triangles over his eyes. A disturbing smile is drawn past his lips, exaggerating his expressions.

He proceeds to taunt Mike and Billy with cruel insults, "How did two scarecrows like you fellas end up scoring these hot chicks?" *Seriously? What's with this weirdo?*

"For starters, we skipped right over the makeup aisle where your blue eyeshadow came from," Billy says.

The clown rolls his eyes. "Here, I'll make you a deal. If either of you tools can dunk me, I won't take these pretty ladies home with me tonight." I cringe at the thought.

"I'll take that bet," Mike says with a sexy confidence like I've never seen. He grabs a ball and lines up with the target. He winds up and pitches the ball with all his might. It zips through the air, beaming into the center of the target.

The clown plunges feet first into the water with a loud splash. He resurfaces a moment later, his smeared makeup running down his face as he gasps for air. "Beginner's luck. I bet your lady friend won't be so lucky," he huffs, climbing aboard his platform again.

"Would you like to try?" Mike asks me, holding out another ball.

"No, thanks." I lean into his ear and whisper, "He kind of creeps me out." Mike nods, ever understanding.

"Or…we could get our fortunes read!" Carla exclaims, pointing to a mysterious black tent standing lonesome and ignored. The four of us head toward the quiet tent. A large red hand comes into view on one flap of the fabric. Above it reads: *Miss Sveta - Psychic Adviser.* We step inside and it is dark and cool, the low hum of a rickety fan the only sound we hear. A dim string of lights is tacked to the ceiling and burning spices perfume the air.

A beaded curtain rustles and a plump, pink-suited woman pushes through from a back room. "You are a phony and completely unprofessional! I want to speak to your manager this instant!" she scolds, holding up a knobby-knuckled finger.

From behind the curtain, we hear another voice—heavy-accented, "You are looking at her, lady! I read what I see. Sorry for you. Not all readings are good."

"I demand a full refund!"

"Sorry, service already been rendered."

The pink lady staggers backward a few steps, looking as if she might faint. Her chubby cheeks now matching the shade of her hot pink suit. She yanks out a bejeweled cell phone from the depths of her large bosom and pokes furiously at the screen. She barks into the phone, "You won't believe what just happened to me!" She bustles by us and out of the tent, her pig-nose turned up to the sky, jabbering at the poor person on the line.

The lady behind the thick accent comes through the curtain to greet us. "Sorry about the crazy lady. It's not my fault her husband's a pig." We all exchange a look before forcing nervous smiles at the frizzy-haired fortune teller standing before us. "Who wants to go first? And no refunds!" she says.

Mike turns to me. "I think Billy and I might sit this one out. Do you girls mind if we head next door to play some games and meet you after?"

"That sounds like fun. I think I'll come with you," I say.

"No! Please, I really want someone to do this with me," Carla begs. *This is a bad idea. What if this lady can see that I'm not human?* But Carla's pleading eyes get the best of me, and I think of the pink lady's sentiments that Miss Sveta is probably a phony, and this is all for show. *Humans don't have Offerings, after all.*

I finally agree to stay. "Okay."

After we pay the woman, Mike gives me a quick kiss. "Have fun you two," he says, before exiting with Billy.

"The spirits don't like to be kept waiting. Who is going first?"

"I will," Carla volunteers enthusiastically. I take a seat on the crimson couch of velvet in the waiting room and watch Carla disappear behind the curtain.

"Ahh!" I jump back in my seat as a black ball of fur pounces onto the empty cushion beside me. The fluffy, jet-black cat has oversized amber eyes. His flattened face looks as if it has been smacked by a closing door several times, yet his snout remains visibly moist. "Shoo!" I whisper. It hisses and arches its back at me before jumping down and sneaking into the back.

Soon, Carla is bouncing back out to me, blathering about her favorable reading. "OH MY GOD, I'M GETTING MARRIED!"

"You are?" I ask.

"Sveta saw me standing under a beautiful waterfall and I have always wanted to honeymoon in Fiji. Oh wow, I wonder when Billy's going to ask me. He's probably already talked to my dad; I bet that's why he was so irritable this morning!"

"Ahem." Sveta clears her throat, glaring at us through the beaded curtain. "Come on, honey. I started your time five minutes ago." I jump up and follow her into the back. There is a small, round table draped with black velvet cloth centered in the room. We take a seat across from one another. A clear ball of glass rests on the table between us, and the spooky cat is now curled up at Sveta's feet.

A lone bookshelf is the only other piece of furniture in the room. Old, dusty books and bottles filled with murky liquids clutter the shelves. I turn my attention back to Sveta. The old woman stares back through eyes webbed with cataracts. A sheer, flowy shawl with fringing is wrapped around her shoulders. "I'm Jane," I say, breaking the uncomfortable silence.

"SHH!" the wrinkled woman hisses. She shuts her eyes and produces a raspy hum. Raising her hands to her sides, she gyrates in her seat. The gold bangles on her arms clatter together with her absurd movements. I cower in fear. *This woman is insane.*

Suddenly, her humming ceases and silence fills the room. I stiffen in my seat. Sveta's eyes shoot open, and she sighs. "Alright, just need to get the spirits stirred up a bit. Just a minute." She rubs her hands together. "Let's try this," she says, getting up and walking over to her bookshelf. She rummages carelessly, tossing books to the floor. "Aha. There you are my trusty sage." She pulls out the wrapped bundle and lights the end until white smoke streams from it. This strange woman begins to prance around the room, wafting her sage and mumbling chants under her breath. *This is getting ridiculous.*

Returning to the table, Sveta places the smoking sage on a tray and sits back down. I wave my hand in front of my face and choke back a cough. "Give me your hand," she demands.

I ease my hand out and she yanks it closer to her. As her long silver fingernail traces my palm, my stomach flip-flops and I am suddenly lightheaded. I lean back in my seat as my vision blackens around my periphery. "Hey, girl! Girl!" I hear her yelling, but her voice sounds far away. I come to as a light slap strikes my slack jaw. "Snap out of it!"

"Wha-What just happened?" My voice trembles, struggling to form a sentence.

"Probably too much sage, dear. Must be allergic. Now get out! We're closed."

"But…what about my fortune?"

"I couldn't read you since you started jerking around like a fool," she says. "The spirits are tired. That's all for today," she continues, pushing me out through the beaded curtain.

My temples throb with a pulsing pain. Something bubbles up from the pit of my stomach. It surges up my throat. I dash for the nearest portable bathroom, running past a concerned Carla to hurl into the toilet. *That feels better.* I wipe my mouth with a paper towel and exit the bathroom. Carla waits for me outside. "Are you okay? What did she tell you?" she asks.

"Yeah, I'm fine. Just a migraine, but I'm starving. Let's go find the guys and get some food."

Mike is holding a teddy bear twice his size when we find him next to the ring toss booth with Billy. "Whoa. Did you win that, Mikey?" Carla asks him.

"Yep, with my bare hands." He turns to face me. "You like it, babe?"

"It's so soft," I say, grazing my fingers over its brown fur.

"Don't worry, I won you something too, babe," Billy says. From behind his back, he pulls out a clear bag with a sad orange fish submerged in a splash of water.

"What am I going to do with a goldfish?" Carla asks. Billy shrugs, defeated.

"If we don't get some food soon, he's gonna be my dinner," I groan, my stomach growling mercilessly. After raiding the concession stand, we sit down at a picnic table. My eyes dart around the spread. Blue wisps of cotton candy, a powdered funnel cake, and a sticky caramel apple—all to be washed down with a huge cola. *Yum!* I scarf down everything in front of me, and a couple handfuls of Mike's boiled peanuts. The loudest burp escapes my mouth. "Excuse me," I say, embarrassed.

Mike giggles. "That's my girl," he says, patting me gently on the back.

"Are you eating for two, Jane?" Carla asks, critical of my cheeks bulging with food.

"What? No!" *Is that even possible?*

Carla accepts my response and moves on quickly. "You never told me what your reading was…spill."

"That lady was right—Sveta's definitely a phony. She just blew smoke in my face and then told me the spirits were tired and kicked me out," I say, imitating her accent as best I can.

Carla's face falls. "I hope not. I was really looking forward to Fiji."

I shrug. "Bummer. Are you going to eat your pickle?"

"Ew—no. It's all yours," Carla says, making a sour face. "Maybe you should take a pregnancy test. You guys did just get married," she says, watching me chomp away at the pickle. Mike and I exchange worried glances but say nothing.

On our drive home, he whips into the first gas station he sees. "Be right back," he says, hopping out, and leaving the vehicle running. He returns holding a small box in his hand and passes it to me. "Everything's gonna be okay. I love you," he says, patting my thigh as I read the instructions on the pregnancy test.

"I didn't think it was possible," I whisper, weeping softly. *Why am I crying?* He pulls me across the seat to him, comforting me all the way home.

"I'll be right outside," he says, as I close myself in our bathroom.

Snapping the cap back on the test, I lay it flat on the counter. *I don't feel any different.* I turn to the side and scrutinize my flat belly in the mirror. *I don't look any different.* I sigh and pace the short length of our bathroom. *This is the longest three minutes of my life.* I take a deep breath and peer down at the indicator. *Pregnant.*

THIRTY-FOUR

MY SCREAMS WAKE ME. **I** sit up in bed and pull my knees to my chest, rocking myself. My eyes pool with tears. *No...that is impossible. Duplicity and Augur could never overthrow the Elders. These pregnancy hormones are just giving me bad dreams...or could they be visions?* Mike stirs from my commotion and sits up, wrapping his arms around me. "Did you have another nightmare, babe?"

My hand covers my mouth and my stomach flips, threatening to erupt at any second. I barely make it to the bathroom before expelling its contents. "I hate when you have morning sickness. I always wish there was something I could do for you," he says from the other side of the bathroom door.

"Me, too. But I'll be fine. Be out in a minute." I brush my teeth and move into the kitchen.

"Hungry? You should try to eat something. How's eggs, bacon, and cheese grits sound?" *Barf.* My stomach heaves at the thought.

"Some oatmeal might be better on my stomach," I suggest.

"Good point," he says, turning to rummage through the pantry.

"Ugh. When is this going to end? Every morning, like clockwork. It's awful."

"Mom said it should be over by the second trimester. Hopefully, you only have a few weeks left." My appetite returns when Mike sets the steamy bowl in front of me. I clear it and even go back for seconds. "Don't forget we have the OBGYN appointment in an hour." There's a trace of excitement in his voice.

I shake my head. "I completely forgot."

"Forgetfulness is a common symptom of pregnancy. Don't sweat it. I'm just so excited we get to see our baby today." Mike grins as he scrubs the dishes in the sink.

"What if they realize the baby is only half-human? Aren't you worried about that?" He rinses the plates in hand and sets them on the dish rack. Then he turns to face me, drying his hands with a dish towel.

"Look at me," he says, holding up both of his hands and taking a seat next to me at the table. "Now look at you." He takes both of my hands in his, turning them over to inspect them. "Do you think anyone would question that we belong together?"

"Well, no…"

"Since you have lived among us, has anyone ever doubted your humanity?"

"No…but you told me they run some tests."

"Nothing like that. Besides, your DNA is probably very similar to ours, how else would you look so much like us?"

"DNA?"

"Don't ask me to explain it because I'm not a scientist." He gazes into my curious eyes. "Oh, alright. Hang on a second." Mike performs a quick search on his phone. "*New Hartford American Dictionary* defines it as 'a self-replicating molecule found in cells that carries the genetic information needed for the development, growth, and reproduction of all living organisms.' Happy?"

"I have no idea what you just said."

He shrugs. "Me neither."

"I'm just afraid, Mike. I don't want anything to happen to the baby."

He looks deep into my eyes, squeezing my hands tightly. "I will do everything in my power to keep the two of you safe. I promise."

I feel the lines of worry on my face soften. "You're right. I shouldn't be so worried. And thank you for breakfast, it was delicious." I pick up my bowl to bring to the sink, but Mike takes it from me.

"I got it, babe," he says, kissing me on the forehead.

"I love you," I say, now feeling the anticipation of getting to see our baby for the first time. I twist my hair and clip it tightly to the back of my head. I slide on a pair of loose-fitting jeans and a baggy T-shirt before we hurry out the door.

The OBGYN waiting room is packed with other women and their big bellies. The salmon-colored walls have a panel of baby-themed wallpaper with pink and blue rattles under the ceiling's crown molding. A middle-aged woman with sharp, magenta lips sits behind the counter sorting through patient charts. She looks up at us with a smile. A few stains from her outdated lipstick have settled on her teeth. "Good morning, please sign in on the clipboard," she says.

Mike grabs the pen and writes "Jane Anselmo" on the next open line, along with my appointment time and doctor's name. "Let me get your paperwork ready since you're a new patient," the woman says. She hands us a clipboard with a small stack of papers clipped to it and a pen. We take a seat on a comfy sofa as I skim over the packet. I improvise most of my answers, asking Mike for help occasionally.

"Okay, I think that's everything," I say, handing the clipboard back to the woman.

"Alright, Mrs. Anselmo, now I just need to make a copy of your ID." I hesitantly hand the card to her, hoping she doesn't question it. The woman stares at it and then back at me, squinting her left eye as she looks it over. Little beads of sweat run down the back of my neck as I wait for her to finish examining it. "You're really photogenic," she finally says. I exhale into an uneasy laugh as she hands my ID back to me.

I glance it over once myself, looking for any discrepancies that could tip someone off to my true identity, even though I know it's just my paranoia. This ID is as authentic as it comes, printed straight from the DMV after we got our marriage license.

My name reads as Jane Anselmo and my photograph captures the awkward stare inherent to those of human identification cards. But when I gaze upon the address line, my mouth hangs open. After all this time, it finally hits me. The ranch is located at 412 SE Tibbetts St. Cougar, WA 98616. The exact wording of Mother's bizarre prophecy from all those years ago. *Whoa.*

"I'll get this paperwork inputted right away, but I'm also going to need to collect a sample from you. The bathrooms are down the hall to your left. When you're finished, just place the cup in the little metal window, and then you may return to your seat until we call your name." She hands me a clear, empty cup with a light blue lid twisted on it.

I am confused. "A sample of what?"

"A urine sample…to verify that you are pregnant, dear."

"Oh…okay. So, I just pee in the cup? And then place it in the window?"

"Yes, ma'am. Then come back out to the lobby and we'll call you back in a few minutes once we've checked the results." I take the cup and go into the bathroom. I fill it awkwardly and eye the warm liquid. *Gross.* My face tightens, wondering what else they will be able to detect from the sample. I tremble and place the cup in the metal window before returning to the waiting room.

"Is everything alright? You don't look so good," Mike says.

"Yeah, I'm just nervous," I whisper.

He gently rubs my small baby bump. "I know you're scared, but everything is going to be okay."

A waif of a young woman in teal scrubs walks into the lobby. Her little bob of blond hair barely clears five feet. "Mrs. Anselmo, we're ready for you," she says. The neon green rubber bands secured around her braces threaten to snap as she speaks. The absurd color makes her overbite impossible to miss.

I force a smile. "Can my husband come with me?"

"Of course. Come on back. We'll be in the first room on the right. Go ahead and hop onto the table and lift up your shirt so I can have access to your belly." The paper crinkles as I slide onto the exam table. I lift my shirt and watch as the girl prepares the equipment. Her name badge informs me her name is Judy. "Do you have any names picked out yet?" she asks.

"I like Titus," Mike says, a little too overzealous.

"That's a nice name. What about you, mama?"

"Oh, I don't know. I don't have a favorite yet. But I think I'll know when I hear it," I say.

The woman nods. "I'm just going to massage some warm gel onto your belly, to help us see the baby. I'll glide this probe along your lower abdomen and if you just watch the screen here, you'll be able to get the first glimpse of your little angel."

I watch through anxious tears as Judy pushes the probe into the gel and slides it around my pelvis. The screen turns bright white. "That's strange. I've never seen that happen before. This equipment was just calibrated. Hold on, let me reposition the probe."

My heart pounds in my chest as the woman glides the probe across my tummy at different angles. Mike and I exchange fearful glances. *I knew this was a mistake.* "Is something wrong?" he asks her.

"There we go," Judy says. A scratchy, black-and-white image comes into view of a tiny head and body. "There it is. Oh wow, look at that activity. I've never seen a baby have so much movement at eight weeks. You might just have a little prodigy on your hands."

"That's our baby?" I ask in awe, smitten with the tiny life that I've never even met. I watch the screen in wonderment as the tiny baby flutters around. An overflowing sense of joy and warmth fills me.

"Yes, ma'am. Now, it's too early to determine the gender, so we will wait awhile for that. But it looks like you have a very healthy baby. The heart rate is slightly above average, but that shouldn't be a problem. It is an old wives' tale that babies with higher heart rates are said to typically be girls," she says, smiling at us.

"As long as it's healthy, I'll be happy either way," I say.

"Okay, so I just took a few measurements of the baby. We're looking at about March 25th for your due date. Congratulations, mom and dad," she says. "Let's print a few pictures of your little one for you to take home. If the little tike would just stay still for a moment...there! That's a good one."

Mike and I smile with damp eyes, hovering around the first picture of our child. "Can you believe it? We're going to be parents!" he exclaims.

THIRTY-FIVE

NOW THAT I'M IN THE final trimester of my pregnancy, I can't go a single night without being haunted by visions of the Fairkind in turmoil. Here I lie again, tossing in bed, drenched in cold sweat. "Remedy! Storm! I'm coming back for you!" I yell out, half asleep.

Mike hushes me as he strokes my damp hair back from my face. "It's okay, babe. Just another dream is all."

"No. Something is wrong," I say, panting.

"Even if that's true, what can you do about it?"

I rub my forehead, thinking. "I don't know."

I follow Mike into the kitchen, and he turns on the griddle. He whisks some ingredients together and pours the mixture over the hot surface. The golden batter sizzles as it assumes the shape of several small discs. "I know you are worried about your friends but try to think about our baby. All this extra stress can't be good for the pregnancy," he says. I nod my head, looking into his worried eyes. *He's right.* I try not to dwell on my fears any longer, which—thanks to my growling stomach—turns out to be much easier than I would've thought. "Besides, after breakfast, I have a surprise for you," he adds.

"Your family sure does love surprises," I mumble, having a seat at our dining table.

Mike places a heaping plate of buttery pancakes before me with a thud. "Do I sense some hostility? If you're gonna be cranky, I'll just go ahead and tell you. I know your back has been hurting and I wanted to send you to get a prenatal massage this morning."

Tears flood my lash line. "You did?"

"Of course, my love," he says, handing me the gift certificate. "I want you to be comfortable. And in a better mood, I might add," he says, poking a gentle finger into my side.

I sigh. "I'm sorry. I don't know what's come over me today."

He kisses me on the cheek. "I'll let it slide this time since you're carrying my baby. Go ahead and eat, though, and I'll order a driver from the car service to pick you up."

"Sounds good to me," I say, drizzling syrup all over the fluffy stacks.

"You know, if you had let me teach you to drive like I wanted, you could have just taken my truck."

"Nope. Not happening." I shake my head. "I'm happy to ride with a driver."

"Whatever you say, babe." He comes around the table to give me a peck on the lips. "I need to go ahead and get to the stables, but I love you. Oh, and before I forget, the paint came in for the baby's room. I figured I would roll it on this weekend."

"That sounds perfect."

"The driver should be here anytime, so keep an eye out." Mike drops to his knees and kisses my round belly. "Goodbye Violet."

"That's not her name," I say.

"Goodbye Sarah."

"I don't think so."

"Amelia?" he asks, the confidence waning in his voice some. I shake my head. "Well, I'm going to continue to call her by a new name until you pick one," he says.

"Fair enough. I love you too," I say. He smiles and he's gone. I have just enough time to squeeze into a pair of sweats and an old T-shirt when I see the unfamiliar car pull up the long drive. I grab my purse and step outside to meet the driver.

The man rolls down the passenger's side window and calls across the seat, "Anselmo?"

"Yes, that's me." The driver says nothing else, just resumes a forward glance. I clamber inside his small four-door and watch him punch something into his GPS. He jams his foot down on the pedal looking uncomfortable with his big belly—even bigger than mine—squashed behind the worn steering wheel. Beads of perspiration sit on the back of his thick neck, just below his lonesome ring of hair resistant to premature balding.

I catch a glimpse of his face in the rearview mirror. His eyes are tired and angry underneath a bushy unibrow. I jerk my eyes back to the road as the engine hums from another abrupt acceleration. We race toward a yellow traffic light in the distance, about ten car lengths away. I brace myself against the car door as we catch air, flying through the red light at the intersection.

"I'm in no rush," I say, nervously. I lean forward to peer into the front seat and spot a silver flask, half-concealed by the man's jacket. "Sir, have you been drinking? Please pull over. I'd like to get out."

The man cackles until it morphs into a phlegmy cough as he swerves in and out of traffic carelessly. "Can't stop now, mama. We're almost there. I must do my job! You don't want to take that away from me too—do you?!" he shouts, then takes a swig from his flask.

Up ahead, railroad crossing lights begin to blink and the gates lower. "We can make it!" the man exclaims, pushing the gas pedal to the floor. We speed around slowing cars toward the oncoming train, racing to clear the tracks.

I reluctantly enter his mind, his troubled thoughts echoing loudly in my head. Such anguish contained in this lone man. I attempt to bend him to my will just as I had practiced in school. *Stop! Stop! Pull over!* But he proceeds on his maniacal way unfazed. *CHOO-CHOOOO.*

"Stop! Please—no—my baby!" I scream.

The train's whistle blares, warning us to back down. But the car drives right through the gate, obliterating it in a wake of splinters. I brace myself again, this time preparing for impact. "We're not going to make it!" I scream.

Right as our car reaches the tracks, the train barrels by, clipping our front end. A deafening crash echoes from the impact on the front corner of the driver's side. We are sent into a violent tailspin, and I feel the immediate cinching of my seatbelt across my chest and lap. Once, twice, three times the car spins, before veering off and flipping into a ditch.

We jolt to a final resting place, and I hear a loud crack as my head bounces against my window. I wince expectantly but feel no pain. The window is left scored into an intricate web. Glass shards glint as loose slivers fall through a gleam of sunlight on their way to the ground. I trace my fingers along my scalp in search of a corresponding wound but find none.

The back tires continue to whiz behind me, spinning feverishly in the air. The noxious smell of burnt metal permeates my lungs. I groan and try to unbuckle my seatbelt, but it's jammed.

Smoke fills the car, and I cough, squinting to see through the fumes and chaos of an upside-down world. Through the haze, I see the driver motionless in the front seat. A pool of blood gathers under his head, dripping from a large gash in his neck. "Sir, are you okay?" I shout. No response. "Can you hear me?"

I start to panic. "Please, somebody help us! Anybody!" I don't recognize my voice as I beg for help that isn't coming. My head starts to feel heavy from being upside down. I jiggle the door handle, but it is stuck. My mind grows foggy until I can't see clearly anymore.

When I open my eyes again, there is blurred movement. My body suffers the rough jars that can only occur in the rare instance you are being dragged by your arms from the havoc of a wreck. My head is lowered onto the grass and a shadowed face stares down at me. Rays of sun beam from behind the figure, blinding their features. But the voice that comes from the silhouette is that of a man, "Help is on the way, Jane." The simple phrase is soothing and familiar in a way I can't explain.

"Mike...?" my voice cracks.

The man chuckles and shakes his head. "Not quite."

"Who are you?" His face comes into focus, and I am convinced I remember him from somewhere. His hair is dark and piercing green eyes hang above his smooth cheeks.

"That's a story for another time," he says. There is a contagious warmth about him, and I cannot help but return his endearing smile.

Muted voices approach in the distance, and the wails of sirens eventually snap me back to full coherence. A woman in uniform kneels beside me. "You're going to be okay. We're taking you to the hospital. How far along are you?"

"Um...thirty-eight weeks. Wait. Where'd that man go?"

The woman grabs a neck brace and fastens it under my chin. "What man?"

"A man helped me out of the car. I need to tell him thank you."

"The only witness I've seen is the woman who called in to report the crash." She nods in the direction of an older woman off

201

to the side, speaking to a police officer. *That's odd. Where could he have gone so fast?*

"Why do I have to wear this thing around my neck?" I ask, tugging at the brace.

"It's just a safety precaution. Please try to remain calm until we can get you and your baby checked out."

"What about the driver? Is he okay? He's bleeding."

"Unfortunately, he didn't make it." A loud blast reaches our ears and both the paramedic and I flinch as the upside-down car roars into a sudden heap of flames. *He pulled me out of there just in time.* My head begins to pound as I breathe in the burning fuel on the wind. The paramedic turns to face me with her stunned expression still in place. "Wow. You really are lucky to be alive. It must be *kismet.*"

"What did you say?" I ask.

The woman leans in closer and raises her voice, "I said it must be KISMET." My belly flutters with the sudden rolls and kicks of my baby. The EMTs strap me onto a stretcher and load me into the back of an ambulance. The woman jumps in behind me, taking my vitals and writing notes on a clipboard. "Ma'am, can you tell me your name, please?"

"It's Jane—" I recoil automatically as a cramp tightens in my lower back. The sharp pain strikes all the nerve endings along the column of my spine. "Jane Anselmo," I sputter.

The woman calls out to the driver, "She's having a contraction," and a sudden burst of fluid runs down my legs. "Your water just broke. You're in labor," she informs me.

"I am?"

"Yes, ma'am. It looks like you'll be meeting your little one very soon," she shouts over the blaring sirens as we speed toward the hospital. *But am I ready to be a mother?*

THIRTY-SIX

A S COMFORTABLY AS THE CONTRACTIONS allow, I settle into my bed at the hospital. I search for the source of the repetitive beeping, inspecting the various cords I am plugged up to. The pestering noise isn't exactly soothing the sharp cramping in my abdomen. But soon the magical epidural kicks in to relieve the sensations of pain, just as the nurses promised.

Mike has been made aware of the situation by the hospital staff, and he assured them that he is on his way. While I wait for him to arrive, I can't shake the feeling of familiarity I experienced with the mystery man who helped me to safety after the collision. I try to retrace my experiences, taking a mental inventory of people I've met and spoken to since arriving in Washington. *He isn't someone I know from the land of humans, of that much I am certain.*

Those eyes—those deep green eyes are unforgettable…

Mike bursts through the heavy door. "Are you alright? How's the baby?"

"We're fine. A tad traumatized, but everything seems to be okay. The nurses keep telling me it's a miracle," I say, propping myself up in the bed.

Mike takes a seat at my bedside, tilting my chin to the left and right. "You look pretty darn good for having been in a major car crash. I don't see a scratch on you!"

"Yeah, we got lucky. I'm just glad our baby girl is okay."

"Me too. Oh, and I brought your hospital bag," he says, placing the duffle bag in a chair in the corner. "So, how long before we get to meet her?" he asks excitedly.

"They say it could still be a while." A smile spreads across my face. "But I did decide on a name today."

"You did?"

"What do you think about Kismet?"

"Kismet," he tries it on. "It's perfect."

"Where's your mom and dad?" I ask, munching on ice chips.

"I hate to ruin the surprise, but part of the reason I sent you for a massage was so that they could secretly set up for your baby shower."

"Another surprise? It's too much, Mike," I say, laughing.

"Yeah, I know. Anyway, they're working on rescheduling with all the guests at the moment. They will be here as soon as they can. How are your contractions?"

"Not too bad. They gave me an epidural right before you got here, so now I hardly feel them at all."

"I'm glad to hear it. Do you need any more ice chips?"

"Maybe in a little bit. I might try to take a nap. I'm pretty tired."

"Yeah. Get some rest, babe. I'll be right here when you wake up." I close my eyes and doze off.

"Mrs. Anselmo?" The midwife nudges my arm.

"I'm awake," I yawn.

"Alright, we should be getting close. I need to do a quick check." I wiggle with discomfort as the woman examines between my splayed legs. "You're nine centimeters dilated. One more to go. Then it's time to push." I start to panic because Mike is no longer in the room, and I'm terrified to do this alone. "I'm going to get the doctor and some supplies. I will be right back," the nurse says, discarding her gloves. She adjusts the stethoscope hanging from her neck and disappears into the hallway.

I practice the pursed-lip breathing the nurses taught me because my heart threatens to break through my chest. *Where is my husband?* Through the door steps a huge arrangement of pink flowers. Mike's head pops out from behind the petals. "Oh, good. You're awake."

Worry lines his face as he watches me struggle to breathe. "It's time," I say between breaths. The door swings open and my nurse is back along with a man in a white coat. She rolls in a table full of supplies and begins setting up. Mike drops the flowers on my bedside table and stands at attention next to me.

"Hello, Mr. and Mrs. Anselmo. I'm Doctor Ramey and I hear we're about ready to go." He guides my feet into a set of stirrups not unlike the ones found on the saddles back at the ranch, but I am placed in the most awkward position imaginable, completely exposed. The doctor snaps on a fresh pair of gloves and says, "Let's have a baby."

"I'm scared, Mike. I don't think I can do this," I say, weeping.

He grabs my hand and, with his other, turns my face toward him. "You are the bravest woman I know. You can do anything."

I smile a little, nodding my head. "I'll try," I squeak.

"Okay, Mrs. Anselmo. I need you to push for me," Doctor Ramey says. I take a deep breath and bear down with all my might. "That's good. Keep pushing." I push for as long as I can until I have to breathe again. "You're doing great, Jane. Rest for a minute and then we'll go again."

Mike is whispering in my ear, "You're amazing. I love you," and it gives me the strength I need when the doctor tells me it's time to push again. The pressure is almost unbearable, and each push feels like it lasts a lifetime.

"We're almost there, Jane. We just have to get past the shoulders. I need you to give me your biggest push yet."

A guttural scream tears from my lips as I push with every ounce of strength I have left. And then, suddenly, the immense pressure releases and a tiny cry fills the room. My heart bursts at the sound. "Congratulations," the nurse says, placing my dainty daughter on my chest. Her cries cease as soon as her skin presses into mine. *I have never loved anyone more in my entire life.*

"Would you like to do the honors, dad?" Doctor Ramey asks, handing a pair of scissors to Mike.

"Absolutely." Mike cuts the cord proudly and beams back at us.

Kismet has the most extraordinary wisps of white-blond hair and Mother's nose. She coos in my arms as her eyes slit open to gaze upon the world for the first time. *And Mike's eyes.*

A soft, crinkled hand reaches out and latches onto my pointer finger. She grips tightly around it, as if she already knows exactly who I am. I cannot get enough of her velvety folds and wrinkles. Or those perfect pink lips that are begging to be smothered with kisses. I bend down and, ever so lightly, plant a sweet one on her teeny lips. "You are so beautiful, Kismet. Mommy loves you very much," I whisper softly, tears streaming down my face.

"Alright, mama. I need to take the baby for just a minute to get some measurements and then she'll be all yours. Do you have a name picked out?" the nurse asks.

I gently hand over my bundle of joy. "Her name is Kismet."

"Kismet. That's a beautiful name. It suits her." The nurse places her in a rolling bassinet and wheels her toward the door.

Mike squeezes my shoulder. "You did it. Our beautiful baby girl is perfect."

"I know. I love her so much already."

"I can't wait for my parents to see her. Did I tell you they're out in the waiting room? They texted me. I should go check in with them soon."

"I'm glad they made it."

"How are you feeling? Any pain?" he asks.

"I'm fine, just feeling exhausted. Do you think it'd be alright if I rested my eyes for a few minutes until they bring her back?"

"Of course, babe. I won't leave your side."

I'm so tired that I ignore the wet puddle pooling underneath me and let myself drift far away. A frantic beeping pierces through my dream state but it's distant from me. Mike's muffled shouts find their way to my ears, but I'm too drowsy to reply.

Then a louder voice calls to me, a voice I've been missing for so long. It belongs to Mother. She takes a seat beside me on a log in an iridescent forest, clear as day. "My beautiful daughter, I've missed you," she says.

"Mother." I reach for her, and she pulls me into her warm embrace. Her formerly aged face has been restored to its vibrant youth, even younger than the face I remember. A twinge of betrayal suddenly sweeps over me, and I wiggle free from her grasp. "Artifice? Really?"

"He wasn't always like that."

"You still should've told me."

"Too risky, my sweet girl. Kismet's birth had to be hidden from everyone, even you."

"Well, how did I get all the Offerings? And why did it take so long for me to receive them?"

"Oh, dear, you misunderstand. Your Offering provided a shield of protection over Kismet. I told you, you're very special. So is she."

"A shield of protection? So, surviving the car crash? That was my Offering?"

"Now you're getting it," she chuckles. "And the human fortune teller. You protected Kismet from anyone's discernment your whole life. You thought you never received an Offering when, in fact, you're the first of our kind to receive one at birth. And a brand new one, at that. *Well*, the first since the Fall..." her voice trails off and she shuts her mouth into a tight smile.

"The Fall? Why are there still things you aren't telling me?"

"All in time, dear."

"If what you say is true, then how was I able to do all of these other miraculous things?"

"Those gifts never belonged to you. You merely borrowed them," she states matter-of-factly.

I am astounded by how important my daughter must be. "She really is special, isn't she?"

Mother rises to her feet and holds out a glowing hand to me with another smile. "It's time to come home, Jane."

"But I'm not ready to die."

"Death is a part of life, but it's not the end. Just look at me!" she chuckles. Her laugh wraps around me like a warm blanket. But my heart breaks under the weight of her words.

"What about Kismet and Mike? They need me."

Her face softens and she kisses my forehead. "Kismet will not become who she is destined to be unless she loses you. Greatness can only be forged from adversity. Now come, there's someone I'd like you to meet."

A profound peace rushes over me when I notice the man standing behind us dressed in immaculate white robes. Those green eyes. "It was you," I say. He chuckles and I've never felt so alive, which is strange because I know I am on the verge of death. "I remember you now. You were in our house when I was a small child, talking with Mother."

"Well done, Jane. Few have the courage to start a new life among foreign people as you have done. I had big plans for you, and I have watched them all come to pass with great pleasure. My plans are even bigger for Kismet."

"So, who are you?"

"I have many names," he says. "But I prefer Providence above them all." A pair of magnificent white, feathered wings extend from his shoulder blades, flapping at his sides. "Come now, there is much to tell."

END OF BOOK ONE

To support Randolph Kuczer:

REVIEW THIS BOOK ON AMAZON AND GOODREADS.

Every review helps new readers discover *The Fairkind*.